WIN HADLEY SPORT STORIES

WINNING PITCHER (*A baseball story*)

"KEEPER" PLAY (*A football story*)

OVERTIME UPSET (*A basketball story*)

SET POINT (*A tennis story*)

SLASHING BLADES (*A hockey story*)

DUEL ON THE CINDERS (*A track story*)

A Win Hadley Sport Story

"KEEPER" PLAY

BY MARK PORTER

SIMON AND SCHUSTER

New York, 1960

LIBRARY OF CONGRESS CATALOG CARD NUMBER:
60–8130
MANUFACTURED IN THE UNITED STATES OF AMERICA
BY H. WOLFF BOOK MFG. CO., INC., NEW YORK

CONTENTS

CHAPTER		PAGE
1	Football Season Again	7
2	Coach Joyce Finds His Play	13
3	Bad News from Walt	25
4	A New Star Is Born	37
5	A Jealous Plotter	50
6	Dan's Grandstand Play	62
7	Beat Those Bulldogs!	75
8	Walt's Big Deal	86
9	An Ultimatum	95
10	Ups and Downs	104
11	Win Shows His Stuff	125
12	Thief in the Night	137
13	A Nose for News	151
14	A Wrong Righted	164
15	Victory Play	172

CHAPTER ONE

Football Season Again

WHOOOOEE!

The sound of the quitting-time whistle echoed shrilly through the cavernous confines of the Slade Sawmill Company, and Win Hadley paused involuntarily at his job of stacking freshly sawed planks on the loading platform. Then, slightly embarrassed at his eagerness to be through, Win bent his dark, close-cropped head to the job again. Might as well get it done, he told himself. Only a few more minutes' work won't hurt me.

So Win carefully stacked the remaining dozen planks and then, running his hand over the pile to make sure they were all firmly and neatly placed, he turned, seized the shirt he had discarded when the September sun reached its midday warmth, and hurried off to the washroom.

"Step on it, Win," a voice beside him said, "or

they'll be finished playing before we get there."

Win Hadley nodded in agreement with Matt Hughes, his closest friend, and quickly began soaping his hands and sloshing water over his face to remove the fine film of sawdust that had settled over his straight, strong features.

"Boy," Matt Hughes went on, slipping into his shirt, "am I ever glad that today's the last day of work!" His face darkened. "If only that didn't mean that Monday was the first day of school."

"First day of football practice, too, Matt," Win said, smiling, and Matt Hughes's good humor returned to him instantly.

"Gee, I'd almost forgot! Wonder if Coach Joyce will let me play end this year. He promised me, you know!"

Win Hadley straightened and ran an admiring eye over his friend's stocky, muscular body. He shook his head.

"If he does, he ought to have his head examined. You're the strongest man on the squad."

Matt's face fell and Win smiled inwardly. How easy it was to read Matt's mind. Everything he felt was immediately evident on his handsome, open face.

"Is being strong a drawback?" Matt asked. "Heck, I'm as fast as most of the other ends—and I can catch passes too. That's not counting what I can do on the defense, either. I'm not boasting, Win, but—"

"Of course you're not, Matt," Win put in, throwing an arm about his friend's wide shoulders. "But the one thing we're going to need this year is somebody with some strength in the center of the line."

Matt shrugged. "I suppose you're right. But I sure would like to play end." He grinned impishly, flashing his famous dimples. "You know, I'd like to get my name in the paper, too. People are getting tired of reading about the great Win Hadley and the flashy Dan Slade. Why, I've got it all fixed up with George Slocum. According to our old friend, Scoop, every touchdown scored by a lineman is worth four scored by a back, so you see, I've just got to play—"

"All right, all right!" Win shouted in mock horror, placing a playful hand over Matt's mouth. "If we don't outscore Crawford this year, at least we'll be able to outtalk them! C'mon, let's get our pay envelopes and get going over to the field."

Matt nodded, and they left the washroom and made for the paymaster's window near the Slade Company's exit gate. They got on line, waited their turn, and then drew their final pay of the summer.

"So long, boys," the paymaster, Mr. Wilkins,

called out to them as they turned and headed for the gate. "See you next summer, I hope."

Matt and Win waved friendly hands and were about to call out in reply, when a level voice, full of easy authority, cut them short.

"I'll second that, Mr. Wilkins," the voice said. "I certainly will be happy to see them back next summer."

The boys turned and saw Owen Slade, the president and owner of Slade Sawmill Company, Dixboro's biggest industry, advancing toward them. He was a big man. Though he was now a trifle heavy, the lightness of his carriage suggested strength and a highly successful athletic career when he was a youth. His hair was gray at the temples, and his face, usually set and sober, was now glowing with a warm smile as he came up to them.

"Goodbye, Win, goodbye, Matt," he said, shaking both their hands. "Certainly sorry to see you go. But then, Coach Joyce will certainly be glad to see you come."

Noting with approval how both boys flushed in embarrassment, Mr. Slade quickly changed the subject.

"Dan's back in town, boys. Probably out at the field right now. He's looking forward to the football season, too."

"We'll need him, sir," Win said. "Dan sure can run those ends."

Mr. Slade smiled. "Yes, and I hope he's in as good shape as you boys are. You know, swimming and boating are good exercise, but wrestling lumber in a mill yard is pretty hard to beat for hardening muscles." He ran his eyes over the frames of both of them. "I know, because that's how I got my start." Mr. Slade glanced at his watch. "Well, I've got more work in the office, boys. Goodbye again, and remember—I mean that about next summer."

With a wave of his hand, Mr. Slade turned and left them, and then, Win and Matt were walking quickly through the gate and hastening down the highway toward Dixboro. As they walked, Matt Hughes cast a sidelong glance at his friend, and said, "Why did you say that about Dan Slade, Win? I mean, about running the ends?"

"Because it's true."

"Yes, but that's the trouble. All Dan wants to do is run the ends. He wants to carry the ball on every play—hog all the glory—and on defense the only thing he wants to do is intercept passes or return punts."

Matt's face was dark with anger again, and Win Hadley laid a restraining hand on his friend's arm.

"Come on now, Matt—don't get worked up

about him. I know he's kind of a grandstander, but he isn't all that bad."

"He is, too," Matt said doggedly. "That's why I wondered about your saying that. I'd have told Mr. Slade something different!"

"No, you wouldn't have, Matt," Win said gently. "That would hurt him, and you wouldn't have done that."

"But somebody should tell him!" Matt burst out fiercely. "That Mr. Slade is one of the finest men I've ever met and I think it's rotten that his son should be a spoiled brat like Dan Slade! Somebody should—"

Matt Hughes never finished his sentence, for both boys had heard the sound that was dearest to their hearts and, hearing it, had suddenly broken into a run. The noise that they had heard was the dull *thud* of shoe leather meeting pigskin. They drew breath, sucking the early autumn air into their lungs, and their nostrils wrinkled as they ran right through a cloud of pungent smoke drifting upward from a pile of burning leaves beside the way.

It was football season again!

CHAPTER TWO

Coach Joyce Finds His Play

YES, it was football season again—and that explained the worried wrinkles on the forehead of Coach Tom Joyce. His normally good-humored face was grave as he walked along Center Street in the direction of the Dixboro High athletic field. As he walked, he ran a worrying hand over his thatch of curly, iron-gray hair, and his long easy strides seemed to shorten each time a particularly unpleasant thought struck him.

One new play, he told himself, shaking his head vigorously. One new play with a lot of switches running off it—that's all I need. I've just got to have deception in my attack this year. Why, those boys from Crawford High must outweigh my lads by fifteen pounds to a man. And Bedloe High and Wharton Tech are supposed to be big and powerful this year, too.

My boys are fast, of course, and they don't lack for heart. And I've got Dan Slade at half to turn the ends and the Hadley boy as the T-formation quarterback. But without a line to open holes, where can my backs run? I'll bet I have the best passer in the Western Massachusetts Scholastic League in Win Hadley, but how much protection can we give him against those charging Crawford linemen?

Coach Joyce struck his fist into his palm with a loud, smacking sound, and he let out a long sigh. One good trick play, he repeated silently—that's the thing we need to make up what we lack in power. He turned into the path leading through the athletic-field gate and his pace and his heart quickened as he, too, heard that familiar *thud* and the sharp, excited cries of high school boys playing football.

They were out on the green oval of the football field and Coach Joyce saw that they were playing touch-tackle. Since Dixboro High's first football practice was still a few days off, awaiting the opening of school, and since League rules forbid a coach to start training his boys until that date, Coach Joyce stood and watched the game from a distance.

One of the teams was putting the ball in play. The center pass went to Dan Slade, who dropped far back as though to throw a long one to lanky Al Jacobson sprinting down the side lines. Then, as the other team's linemen rushed him, Dan faked a throw, tucked the ball under his right arm and went tearing wide around them. He executed a neat side step as one of the touch-tacklers lunged at him with both hands, skipped away and then dashed all the way down the field for a touchdown.

Joyce grinned. That Slade boy certainly can scamper, he thought, even if he does seem a trifle spoiled by his father's money. Then the coach frowned. But if that had been real tackle, not just two-handed touch, and those sand-lot linemen had been the big boys from Crawford or Wharton Tech, Dan Slade probably would have been nailed for a fifteen-yard loss.

He shrugged and returned his attention to the game.

Coach Tom Joyce's eyes nearly started from his head!

The other team had run the kickoff out to the 30, and now Win Hadley was crouching under the center in the quarterback spot. Even though Win had his back to him, Coach Joyce found it easy to recognize his tall, wiry, graceful form. Suddenly, Win took the ball. He started backward, seemed to trip, and then began running along the line to his right. As he did, Matt Hughes went straight downfield from his end position and stubby Teddy Scholari started wide a few yards out from Win Hadley.

Coach Tom Joyce's eyes bugged because he saw the sudden collapse and confusion of the defense. As he said later to his assistant coach, Jocko Williams, "Those poor kids didn't know whether to stop, start—or holler for hamburgers!"

For as Win Hadley galloped behind the line, his head high and his sharp eyes eagerly sweeping the field of play, the football hugged in close to his waist, the other boys did not know whether to defend against a pass from Win to Matt Hughes, a run by Win, a lateral by Win to Dan Slade, or, with Dan then holding the ball, a run by him or a pass to Matt. In a single instant, the delirious coach saw the answer to his prayers. Even as he saw Win fake a pass to Matt and pretend to lateral to Dan, the coach rocked back on his heels and roared an order that gave the newborn play its name.

"Keep 'er!" he shouted.

And that was exactly what Win Hadley did. Having split the defenses by his expert faking with the ball, he suddenly slashed inside the end and took off. He raced all the way down to the 10-yard line before the speedier Dan Slade was able to overhaul him and plant a none-too-gentle two-handed "touch" on Win's back.

It was, in fact, a shove—and it did not go unnoticed by the other boys. Especially Matt Hughes. As Win went sprawling to his knees, Matt came running over, his teeth clenched and his face white with rage. He grabbed Dan Slade by the back of his shoulders and spun him around.

"You spoiled brat!" he gritted. "That was no touch-tackle; that was a shove! You pushed him on purpose."

Win Hadley leaped to his feet to intervene. He got himself in between Dan and Matt, but Dan Slade pushed him aside, and with a contemptuous sneer around his mouth, said to Matt, "Supposing I did push him on purpose? What will you do, Hughes?"

For answer, Matt Hughes gave a low growl and drew back his powerful right arm. But his intended right hook was never thrown. Matt felt a far stronger hand than his close around his biceps and felt himself being turned around.

"That'll be all of that, Matt," Coach Tom Joyce said sternly. "I'll admit you may have your reasons, or at least think you have them—but there won't be any fighting around here while I'm coach."

"Coach!" somebody yelped, and they all wheeled and saw little George Slocum running toward them, waving his arms and yelling as he came. "Coach!" he yelped again. "You'd better get out of here, Coach. Hurry! If you're caught—"

"Hey, Scoop," Al Jacobson shouted, noticing the paper and pencil that George held in one of his hands. "Have you finally blown your top, old scribbler?"

Everybody began to laugh, but in the next instant, the smiles were wiped from their faces and it was George Slocum who might have laughed as Coach Tom Joyce hastened to follow his suggestion to "clear out."

"It's against the League rules, Coach!" George panted as he came running up to them all. "You're not supposed to be anywhere near the team, or else you'll be disqualified from coaching for the rest of the season."

There was a general gasp, and then everybody began talking at once.

"Aw, that's silly, Scoop—Coach wasn't doing any coaching, anyway."

"Even if he was, who's to know?"

"Go on, Scoop—you're just trying to make a story for the school paper."

"That's ridiculous. Everybody knows Coach Joyce would never break the rules on purpose."

But it was Coach Joyce himself who held up a hand and stopped all of the smart remarks at the expense of George Slocum.

"He's right, boys. I shouldn't be here, and I'm leaving right away. But before I do," he said grimly, turning to Dan Slade and Matt Hughes, "I want to get one thing straight. And that is simply that a team means teamwork and when two boys on the same team get to squabbling, that's the end of teamwork and the team. So, now, you two," he went on, looking Matt and Dan Slade squarely in the eye, "I want to see you two end your differences right here and now." Coach Joyce paused. Then, in the steely tone that all his "old boys" had learned to respect and obey, he said, "Shake hands!"

There was a moment of strained silence. Matt Hughes and Dan Slade eyed each other in embarrassment. Slowly, awkwardly, Matt brought his right hand up and offered it to Dan, who hesitated a full second before he took it.

"Sorry," Matt mumbled sheepishly, and then the tension disappeared as Teddy Scholari shouted, "C'mon, it's our ball, second down," and with whoops and shouts the game was resumed, with only Coach Joyce and Matt Hughes noticing that Dan Slade had neglected to return Matt's apology.

But Matt soon forgot this slight in the excitement of the game, and as for Coach Joyce, he was so overjoyed at having discovered what he would soon be calling his "keeper" play that he, too, forgot all about it as he hurried from the athletic field and continued his homeward walk.

Meanwhile the game of touch went forward with both sides evenly matched. Win Hadley's side was able to even the score after Win had flipped a short one to Matt Hughes over the goal line, but thereafter, the passing of Win was counterbalanced by Dan Slade's swift, elusive running. By the time the fire-bell in the Dixboro Fire Department's downtown station had clanged the stroke of six o'clock, the score was still tied and the game had ended.

As the overheated, sweat-streaked boys walked from the field, their light sweaters and shirts flung over their shoulders, Dan Slade was at great pains to snub both Win Hadley and Matt Hughes. He grabbed the football, which was his, and ran up to Archie Campbell, Dixboro High's husky center.

"Come on with me, Archie," he called. "I'll give you a ride home. I've got my sport car parked outside."

"Sport car?" Archie Campbell said, raising his sandy eyebrows in surprise. "Have you got a sport car, Dan?"

"Sure," Dan said, with pretended indifference, stealing a backward glance at Win and Matt to see how they were taking the news. "Dad bought me one this summer."

"But you're not old enough to—"

"Sure I am—with my father's consent. Come on, Arch—riding's a lot cooler than walking."

Dan Slade turned squarely around with a triumphant smirk on his face as he made his last remark, but he never got a chance to gloat. Instead, his face flushed with anger as Matt Hughes grinned and said, "It may be cooler riding, Dan, but it doesn't help a halfback's leg muscles any."

"Any time you want to race me, Hughes," Dan burst out angrily, "just let me know." Then he turned to Archie Campbell and said, "You coming with me or aren't you?" Archie Campbell shuffled his feet for a moment. He looked carefully away from Win and Matt, before he bobbed his head eagerly and lumbered off after Dan like a huge, trusting sheep dog.

As Win Hadley and Matt Hughes walked out of the field gate and turned right on Center Street, they all but leaped off the pavement as the roar of a high-powered motor suddenly burst out behind them, and then a sleek white sport car, with Dan Slade behind the wheel, swept past, not two inches from the curb.

"So long, you peasants!" Dan shouted. "See you in the funny papers."

Before they could reply, Dan jammed his foot down farther on the accelerator, the car lunged forward with a still greater burst of speed and the two friends were left alone with the roar of the motor still thundering in their ears.

Win Hadley glanced quickly at his friend and

saw that Matt's jaw was stuck out again and that his blue eyes were shooting sparks. Win couldn't help laughing at the sight of him.

"Oh, come on, Matt—if you lose your temper again it'll be the thirtieth or fiftieth time today."

"Boy, Win, I don't know how you manage to keep yours," Matt said, shaking his head angrily. "Honestly, I try to like the guy. But how can you? Every time you think he's not so bad after all, he pulls some spoiled-brat stunt like that!"

Win Hadley nodded absently, and then, as though he had forgotten the incident, he began to walk more quickly. To Matt Hughes's astonishment, Win suddenly shook his head and muttered, "Poor guy—you can't blame him."

"Poor guy!" Matt shouted. "How can you call Dan Sl—"

"Shhh! I didn't mean Dan. I was thinking of Archie Campbell."

"Oh," Matt said, a note of understanding in his voice. "You mean about Archie's folks having a hard time?"

"Right. I guess that's why he was so eager to ride in Dan's new car. Not that there's any reason he shouldn't, of course. But you could see he was embarrassed about it."

Matt nodded. When he spoke again, his voice was puzzled.

"What made you think of that, Win?"

Win Hadley tried to shrug lightly. "Well, I guess you might say that Archie and I are in the same boat."

Matt Hughes's eyebrows skyrocketed and once again he looked incredulous; and once again Win Hadley had to laugh at the honest concern registered on his friend's face.

"It's not all that bad, Matt," he said. "It's only that it's been ten years since my Dad died. Even though he was one of the best doctors in town, and left Mom fairly well provided for, ten years of taking care of a family can sure cost a lot of money."

"But your brother's working, isn't he?"

"Well, Walt's only been with the auto agency a couple of years. It's been all right this summer, of course, but now that I'm going back to school and not helping with my salary, why—"

"You?"

"Sure. What did you think I was doing with the money?"

"Gee, I don't know, Win. I guess I thought you might be saving it to help with your college education, the way I am."

Win shook his head. "First things first. I just give it to Mom and she uses it wherever it's needed." But then he brightened and slapped his friend on the back.

"Listen, Matt, this is my worry, not yours. Besides, I'm kind of sorry I told you. I don't think it's nearly as bad as I've made it sound."

"I sure hope not," Matt Hughes said as the two boys turned into Elm Street and neared the square, comfortable, old-fashioned house with the wide porch and neatly trimmed hedges where Win Hadley lived.

"Of course it isn't," Win said. He took a short run and leaped the hedge. Whirling, he shot a warm smile at Matt and said, "See you tonight?"

"Okay. I'll be over after dinner."

"Right," Win Hadley said, and turned and went bounding up the porch stairs, three steps at a time.

CHAPTER THREE

Bad News from Walt

THE MOMENT that Win Hadley sat down to dinner with his mother and his brother, Walter, he realized that something was wrong. Though they tried to smile and make little family jokes as they passed the dishes back and forth among them, though Walter, himself once a famous halfback for Dixboro High, made a halfhearted show of enthusiasm for the coming season, Win realized with a sinking heart that something was seriously amiss.

Finally, when his mother excused herself on the pretext of going to the kitchen, and did not return, Win could stand it no longer. He pushed his half-eaten meal away from him and said to his brother, "What's wrong, Walt?"

"Wrong?" his brother repeated, feigning bewilderment. "How do you mean, Win?"

"Please, Walt. I'm sixteen years old. I just

turned my pay envelope over to Mom as I've always done. Don't you think I have a right to know when something's wrong?"

Walter cleared his throat and shot a warning glance at the door through which Mrs. Hadley had disappeared. Whispering, "All right, but don't tell Mom I told you," he cleared his throat loudly and said, "What say we take a walk, Win?"

Nodding, Win arose from the table and followed his brother out onto Elm Street. As he walked along the pavement, listening, he noticed that the leaves of the elms were already tinted with gold.

"It's this way, Win," Walt began. "We all know Dad left Mom comfortably fixed when he died. But that was ten years ago and there were still a few years to go on the mortgage. To make a long story short, Win, that—and something called inflation—just drained the money off like water in a tub. That's one reason why I had to work my way through Holden College. And I couldn't afford to study medicine, as Dad wanted me to do. Now," he said, his lips tightening, "now, today, I thought I had one of our most expensive autos sold. My commission from the deal was something Mom and I were sort of counting on." He shrugged. "But the deal fell through." The two brothers walked on for another minute in deep silence. Then, trying to make light of it, Walt laughed and said,

"That's why you saw Mom and me wearing Halloween masks for faces tonight."

To Walter's amazement, his young brother seemed to be heaving a sigh of relief.

"Gee, if that's all it is, Walt," Win burst out, "I can solve the problem!"

"You? How can you——"

"Simple. I'll just keep on working!"

Walter Hadley came to a dead stop.

"You'll do no such thing?" he shouted, and Win, startled, turned around to peer at his brother through the gathering dusk.

"But, Walter——"

Win's older brother held up a restraining hand.

"Listen, Win," he said, emphasizing his words, "I may be proud of you for saying that, but I won't hear of it. I'm going to see to it that you get at least as good an education as I got." He grasped his brother warmly by both shoulders. "You're staying in school, Win. And you're not working. We'll manage. Besides," Walter went on, half-smiling to himself, "I may be on the trail of something that would mean security for Mom for some time to come."

"Honest, Walt?" Win broke in eagerly. "What is it?"

"Well, I can't tell you yet. I only got wind of it a few days ago. But if it turns out all right, well . . ." Walter Hadley's voice trailed off and he smiled again. "So forget all that nonsense about taking a steady job. Just keep on studying hard and playing hard, Win, and I'll take care of the rest." Walter's grip on his brother's shoulders relaxed and he turned and headed back toward the house. In the darkness both of them could hear footsteps pounding toward them. "Sounds like Matt Hughes," Walter said, laughing. "I don't think anyone else in Dixboro can make the pavement shake like that."

It was Matt, and his voice was alive with excitement, as he said, "C'mon, let's hurry. We'll be late and Coach won't like it."

"Coach?"

"Sure, didn't he call you? He said he was going to."

"Oh, maybe he did. But Walt and I were outside walking. What's up?"

"Coach is having a meeting at his house. He wants all of the returning letter men—you, me, Dan Slade, Archie, Teddy Scholari, Al Jacobson, all of us. He said something about a new offense. Boy, let me tell you, Win, he was really het up about it."

"Okay," Win said, "just let me tell Mom where I'm going." He hurdled the hedge and dashed into the house. In another moment, he was outside again and the two boys were jogging along the flagstoned pavement, their bodies casting huge shadows in the light of the street lamps that had come on only a few minutes ago.

Almost from the moment he had left the athletic field, Tom Joyce's mind had been crammed full of football diagrams. His head was still alive with end runs and off-tackle slants as he sat down to dinner, gulping his food and barely tasting it, responding to his housekeeper's vain attempts at table talk with a series of exasperating grunts and mumbles. Then, refusing coffee, he clattered downstairs to the "Skull Room" he had fixed up in his basement for the express purpose of holding skull sessions with his football players.

Actually, the Skull Room was nothing more than a dozen camp chairs facing a wide blackboard. And on this board, Coach Joyce immediately proceeded to transfer those diagrams that had been running through his head. In an instant, the blackboard was covered with mysterious-looking formulas composed of triangles and circles and crisscrossed with arrows and dotted lines. Seeing them, a foreigner unfamiliar with the American game of football might have thought he had strayed into the laboratory of an atomic physicist.

As Coach Joyce plied his chalk, humming happily away, he heard someone come down the stairs. Then, behind him, an enthusiastic voice said,

"Saaay! That's terrific! Where did you get that idea, Tom?"

Tom Joyce laid down his chalk and turned to greet Jocko Williams, his assistant.

"As a matter of fact, Jocko, I can't really take credit for it. If you want to know the author's name, I guess it would be Win Hadley."

A flashing smile split Jocko's round dark face.

"I might have known," he said. "That Hadley kid knows his football. But you don't mean to say he thought something like that up? Why, this is exactly the sort of thing we've been talking about since the end of last season."

"Right. Actually, Win Hadley didn't think it up. It just came about from his reaction to a bad situation while the boys were playing touch this afternoon."

"And you took it from there."

"Right again. Now, look at this one, Jocko," Coach Joyce began, picking up a long pointer and aiming it at one of the diagrams. Then he cocked an ear to the ceiling and laid the pointer down again. "Too late. I think I hear the boys."

"How could you miss?" Jocko said, grinning as he placed his hands over his ears against the racket of Dixboro High's football letter men clattering down the cellar stairs.

They came into the Skull Room laughing and

talking. There was Teddy Scholari, square and capable, as always neatly dressed with a careful part in his curly black hair. There was Red McGinley, too, and when Jocko Williams caught sight of the gangly youth with the big hands and big nose and the freckles and unruly red hair, he grinned again and said, "How much weight did you put on this summer, Red?"

"Twelve, Jocko," Red said.

"Twelve what?"

"Ounces," Red said, making such a mournful face that the Skull Room rocked to shouts of laughter from the rest of the boys. Little Charley Bantam laughed so hard he fell off his chair and had to be picked up by Ed Walsh, the wiry tackle who played alongside Charley in his watch-charm guard spot. Al Jacobson and Gabby Windham, the holdover right halfback, were shaking with laughter, too.

Finally, after the chuckles had subsided, Coach Joyce ran his eyes over his audience and asked, "Everybody here?"

The answering silence was shattered by the sound outdoors of a high-powered automobile racing around a corner on two screeching tires, followed by the protesting squeal of rubber as the car was brought to a sudden halt.

Everyone present had guessed who the driver of

the car was, and the chuckles began again when Red McGinley drawled, "Sounds like Fancy Dan, the Sport-Car Man."

In another instant, Dan Slade was striding nonchalantly into the room, throwing a careless "Hi, Coach" at Tom Joyce before he dropped into a chair and crossed his legs with a cocky expression on his face. Lumbering after him, red-faced, was Archie Campbell. He mumbled something to the coach and took a seat next to Dan.

For a moment, Coach Joyce's light blue eyes turned frosty. He stiffened, as though preparing some rebuke, but then, changing his mind, he picked up the pointer again and walked to the blackboard.

"All right, boys," he said, "we're going to try something different this year." The pointer came to rest on a diagram like the one given here. "And this is it. Now I want you to study it for a minute and tell me what you think of it."

As Win Hadley studied the play, there was a bewildered expression on his face. But then, he came alight with recognition.

"Why, Coach," he burst out, "this is why you almost broke the League rules this afternoon!"

"Right. I'll have to admit I was a bit excited. Now, listen, boys. None of you fellows except Matt Hughes or Archie there will pretend that he's a heavyweight. You're tough, I know, and

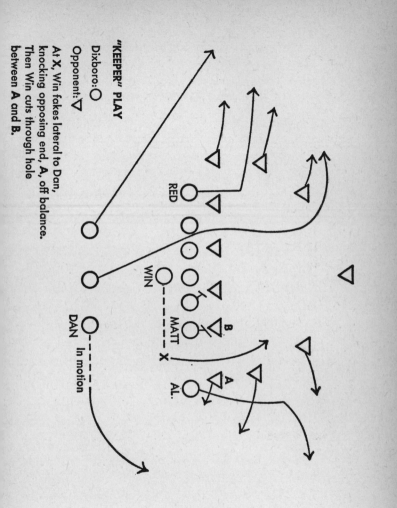

"KEEPER" PLAY

Dixboro: ◯
Opponent: ▽

At X, Win fakes lateral to Dan,
knocking opposing end, A, off balance.
Then Win cuts through hole
between A and B.

RED

WIN

MATT

DAN   In motion

X

AL.

A

B

pretty fast. But we're going to need more than that if we're going to take the W.M.S.L. title away from Crawford this year." He tapped his pointer on the blackboard for emphasis. "This is going to give us that extra something. Now, I want you all to copy these plays and study them over the weekend. After you've got them down, you can start asking questions."

For a full five minutes, there was no sound in the room save for the scratching of pencils on paper. Then Dan Slade spoke up.

"Coach, I guess I'm the back who goes wide to the right."

"You are."

"And the idea is for Win Hadley to suck in the defensive end by pretending to run before he laterals to me?"

"Right again."

Dan Slade smiled and looked around the room with a superior air.

"Well, now we're going somewhere," he said, and sat down.

Coach Joyce studied him.

"It may interest you to know, Dan," he said evenly, "that there are ten other boys on the team." Dan Slade flushed, and then, hearing someone snicker, he glanced around him angrily. "This series of plays is for Dixboro High's football team," Coach Joyce went on. "They aren't for any individual." He picked up the pointer again. "For instance, I expect a lot of passing off it. When Al Jacobson goes downfield from his right-end position, he can either block or move into position to receive a pass. In fact, any of the downfield blockers can become pass receivers. Most important of all, since most of these plays will be going to the right, we are going to need some mighty good protection for the quarterback." He smiled and jabbed the pointer at Matt Hughes. "That means you, Matt."

Matt's face fell and he groaned aloud.

"What's wrong, Matt?" Tom Joyce asked.

"Gee, Coach, you told me that I could play end this year."

Coach Joyce shook his head gently.

"Sorry, Matt. With this offense, I think I'll have to move Red out to left end and put you in at right tackle." Matt Hughes looked so dejected that the coach rushed on to ease his disappointment. "We need your muscles in there, Matt. The whole attack will depend on how you protect our right side. I mean that, Matt."

"I know you do, Coach," Matt said, a droll expression on his face. "But will the fans know it?" Hearing his teammates laugh, Matt made a wry face and wailed, "What am I going to do with that big new scrapbook I bought to keep my newspaper clippings in?"

Coach Joyce joined the general laughter. He was pleased to see Matt taking the change in such good humor.

"That's the spirit, Matt," he said, putting down his pointer. "That's what I want to see from every one of you! Teamwork! If we're going to win the W.M.S.L. this year, we're all going to have to forget our own glory—like Matt here—and get in there and fight! Now, that's all. But, remember, I want you to study these plays over the weekend and be ready to try them out the first thing on Monday."

Then Coach Tom Joyce grinned and added, "Meeting's adjourned in favor of sandwiches and Coke in the kitchen."

With a whoop and scuffling of feet, the room emptied out.

CHAPTER FOUR

A New Star Is Born

"ALL RIGHT, everybody in helmets! Let's go!"

It was the first scrimmage. And no sooner had Coach Tom Joyce walked back to the side lines than Dixboro High's black-shirted Cougars began strapping on their gold helmets as they ran to take up their positions for the kickoff.

This was going to be the first real test of Coach Joyce's new system. For two weeks, now, the boys had been practicing. The linemen had been working out on the tackling and blocking dummies and practicing starts for their offensive charge. The ends had been rehearsing their steps and head feints for receiving passes, or else had been going downfield under Win Hadley's high, spiraling punts to attempt to tackle backs such as Dan Slade before they could get started on the return. Overall, the entire team had spent a week running through dummy scrimmage.

And now, with Coach Tom Joyce blowing shrilly on his whistle, the first real scrimmage was on!

Matt Hughes was doing the kicking off for the Varsity and his powerful leg muscles bunched as his toe met the ball with terrific force. It was a good, high kick—traveling end-over-end to the Scrubs' 5-yard line, where it was caught by their safety man.

He came tearing straight up the middle, running high and looking for an opening. Win Hadley hardly felt the impact of the Scrub tackle who had slammed into his thighs in an attempt to take him out. He shoved him aside quickly and drove straight ahead for the ball carrier. He was spinning away from the clutches of Teddy Scholari when Win left his feet and dived for him. Wham! He had gotten him around the ankles and sent him sprawling on the 21.

The first body contact of the season felt good, and Win scrambled to his feet with the blood singing in his veins.

"Six-two-two-one," shouted Al Jacobson, the defensive signal-caller. Quickly, the Varsity shifted into that type of defensive alignment best for stopping the straight T-formation being used by the Scrubs. To Win's surprise, the Scrub quarter took the snap from the center, took one step backward, and then, leaping high in the air, flipped a jump pass to his left end, slashing inside Win's position. The end took three more steps before he was brought down by Gabby Windham.

Scrubs' ball, second down, two to go!

On the next play, the quarter took another backward step, faked the jump and drove forward between Ed Walsh and Charley Bantam, to ramble for six more yards and the first down.

Sitting on his side-line bench, Coach Tom Joyce nudged Jocko Williams and grinned. "Nice going, eh?" he whispered. "Nothing better for a Varsity than a cocky bunch of Scrubs." Jocko smiled and then turned his attention back to the game. His eyes were on Win Hadley, into whose position the first pass had gone. He began smiling again as he observed Win's tactics.

Stung by that surprise jump-pass, Win now pretended to be careless. He deliberately fell back about two yards, leaving a welcome gap between himself and the Varsity line. Pretending to adjust his shoulder guards, he eyed the Scrub quarter. Good! He had noticed it.

The moment the ball was snapped, Win Hadley charged into the gap he had set as a trap. The Scrub end came dashing down from his position and the quarterback jumped and threw. But Win Hadley got there first. His hands closed around the ball and he made for the side lines. But the disgruntled end nailed him around the waist and dragged him down.

On the bench, Jocko Williams was smiling broadly.

"I knew they wouldn't fool that Hadley kid two times running," he said.

Now it was the Varsity's ball on the Scrubs' 41-yard line.

Back in the huddle, Win barked, "Teddy on a buck over left guard. On *three*."

Dan Slade hissed, "What about the keeper?"

"Not yet, Dan—they'll be expecting it. Let's cross them up, the way they fooled us on that jump-pass."

Dan Slade shrugged and they broke out of the huddle and lined up fast. Win began calling signals.

"One, two, three—"

Archie Campbell slapped the ball into his waiting hands, and Win faked a hand-off to Gabby Windham, who was slamming over from right halfback, before shoving the ball into the belly of Teddy Scholari charging lineward from his fullback slot. As he did, he feigned possession of the ball and began drifting laterally to his right. On the left side of the line, Charley Bantam and Archie had double-teamed the Scrub guard and Teddy burst through the hole. He almost went the distance. But he stumbled as he made a difficult attempt to cut to his left. Still, Teddy had gone twenty yards before they ran him out of bounds. Win grinned. They'd fooled 'em completely.

In the huddle once again, Win said, "Gabby left, on a dive. Count of one."

The Varsity was shouting with glee as the boys ran back to the line of scrimmage and got set. Win felt confident and sure as he crouched under center.

"Signals," he cried. "One—"

The ball was in his hands, Archie Campbell was driving low and left and then Win dived over and slammed the pigskin into the arms of spindle-legged Gabby. And Gabby really took off. He had been hunched low when he hit the line, but meeting no resistance but air, he straightened when he reached the secondary and legged it down to the 5. Win grinned again, jubilant.

In the next instant, his mood changed as Coach Tom Joyce's whistle knifed through the autumn air.

"What's the idea, Hadley?" he called as he walked out on the field. "I thought I told you I wanted you to use the keeper play."

"You did, sir," Win replied. "But I figured they'd be expecting it and decided to cross them up."

Coach Joyce shook his head.

"No. You do what I tell you, son. This is scrimmage, boy, and they don't keep records on scrimmages. You're out here to practice, not to beat the Scrubs." The coach's jaw came out as he barked, "Now, get back there to the 41 and start running that keeper!"

Win Hadley swallowed; he stammered, "I—I'm sorry, sir," and trotted back up the field with lowered head. In the huddle, he found Dan Slade eying him with a mocking grin.

"If you'd listened to me, Hadley," Dan began, speaking with his customary air of superiority, "you'd have saved yourself a tongue-lashing."

"Pipe down and play football," Matt Hughes growled, and Dan whirled on him and snapped, "Who asked you to butt in, wise guy?"

"Quiet, everybody, quiet," Win pleaded. "Now, here it is. The keeper to the right. Al, go down about ten and cut right."

Al Jacobson nodded eagerly, and Dan Slade said, "Who gets the ball?"

"How do I know?" Win answered. "That's the whole point of the keeper. It adjusts to developing situations."

"But you're supposed to lateral to me!" Dan insisted.

"For Pete's sake!" Red McGinley put in. "Is this a football team or a debating society?"

The whistle blew again, and with a backward

glance, Win Hadley saw Coach Joyce pick up the ball and stride off a five-yard penalty for delaying the game.

"You fellows back there better get hold of yourselves soon," Coach Joyce said, a warning note in his level voice. "Or else there's going to be quite a few new faces in the line-up."

Huddling with his team again, Win Hadley at last decided to take off the velvet gloves with Dan Slade.

"All right, listen to me, everybody," he whispered fiercely. "I'm the quarterback and I call the signals! I'm the captain, too, and if I hear one more peep out of anybody I'm sending him out of the game!" He stared at Dan Slade and repeated, "Anybody!" There was a moment of silence while Dan Slade pretended not to be concerned, then Win went on: "All right, same as before, keeper to the right with Al going ten and cutting out. On five. And for Pete's sake, let's take the wind out of those Scrubs' sails."

"Yeah, yeah, yeah!" the Varsity began to chatter as they ran back up to the line of scrimmage; and as Win bent to receive the ball under Archie Campbell he felt the husky center quivering to be off the mark. Win deliberately used a long count to size up the defense. He saw the Scrubs in a five-three-two-one formation, with the trio of linebackers drawn in close. If Al can draw the right-side wingback out of the play, he thought, maybe Dan can scoot down the middle. His count reached five and the ball was in his hands.

Out of the corner of his eye he saw Al Jacobson sprinting downfield and the wingback hugging him close. Running laterally along the line, he saw big Matt holding half the Scrubs' forwards at bay. Now, all he and Dan would have to deal with was the far right linebacker coming over fast. Dan was going wide, calling frantically for the ball. Win faked to him. The linebacker made his move toward Dan, and Win slanted inside.

The linebacker, however, made a quick recovery. He had a clear shot at Win and he launched a diving tackle. But the graceful Varsity quarterback had not shot his bolt. Jumping, Win flipped a basketball pass over the tackler's head—and Dan Slade gathered it in as he hit full momentum and turned the end.

There was no stopping Dan. He went all the way. Al Jacobson had turned to block the man covering him and there was only the safety man between the Cougar speedster and the goal line— and he just couldn't get there in time. It was a 46-yard ramble and Dan was grinning with delight as he circled through the end zone and jogged back upfield to his cheering teammates.

"Now, we're getting somewhere," he called to Win Hadley, completely ignoring the fact that it was Win's expert field generalship and last-second timing that had set him free for his fancy run.

Matt Hughes had a sour expression on his face as he watched Dan being pounded on the back by Archie Campbell and Ed Walsh and Gabby Windham.

"Big grandstander!" he muttered to Win Hadley. "You'd think nobody else but Fancy Dan had anything to do with that touchdown."

But Win was too overjoyed with the success of the play to pay much attention to his disgruntled pal.

"It worked," he kept saying over and over again. "It worked. Oh boy, are we going to have an offense this year!"

Coaches Joyce and Williams were elated, too, but their excitement over Dan's run was almost as nothing compared to their growing jubilation at the way Win Hadley began to run and pass the keeper as the game wore on. Dan Slade was almost forgotten, although it was his presence as a fleet-footed threat on the outside that had much to do with Win's success. Stung by that first long run, the Scrubs had kept a wary eye on Dan, and that gave Win his opportunity.

Next time the Varsity got the ball, Win rifled two straight passes to Al Jacobson, sliced inside tackle for a twisting 22-yard carry, and then amazed even Coach Joyce by actually turning the end himself from 12 yards out. In between, he mixed his plays expertly—sending Teddy Scholari galloping up the middle on short bucks or Gabby Windham diving over tackle. On the only play he lateraled to Dan, the Scrub defenders diagnosed the play and swarmed over the speedy halfback for a 10-yard loss.

Thereafter, it was all Win Hadley and Al Jacobson. Between them, they accounted for four more touchdowns, and by the time the game ended, Dan Slade's mounting hatred and jealousy were at least a match for the rising elation of Coach Tom Joyce. But the veteran gridiron leader was wise enough to conceal his emotions.

"All right, not bad!" he called to the whooping first-stringers. "But, remember, you were only playing your own second team. They just made more mistakes than you did. Twice around the field for everybody, then you can hit the showers and go home!"

In a muttered aside to his assistant, Coach Joyce said, "How did it look to you, Jocko?"

His eyes twinkling, the stubby line coach replied, "If you're asking me, Mr. Joyce, I'd say it looks like Merry Christmas!"

Tom Joyce smiled. "Well," he said, "it's a little early to be passing out season's greetings, but I'd say you've got something there, Jocko."

However, Coach Joyce's enthusiastic estimate of

his team's prospects might have undergone a sober tempering had he witnessed the ugly scene which took place in the locker room only a few minutes after he left the athletic field.

Dan Slade had come out of the showers, streaming water. When he saw Win Hadley seated on the bench in front of his locker, an expression of malicious pleasure came over the halfback's face. He mounted the bench, wrapped only in his towel, and deliberately walked down to Win. When he reached him, he sneered, "Out of my way, glory-boy."

Win Hadley eyed him steadily.

"You know, Dan," he said, "I don't think I'm going to move. And I think you'd better take back that glory-boy wisecrack."

"Why should I?" Dan replied. "After the way you hogged the ball out there today?"

Win Hadley got to his feet. He stared up at Dan Slade. Though his eyes were hard and he gave no outward sign of being disturbed, he was trembling inside. It was not that Win was afraid of a fight. As a matter of fact, there was nothing he would have liked to do more at that moment than to leap up beside Dan Slade and wipe that superior smirk off his face. No, Win trembled for fear he would lose his temper and *do* just that—and that would ruin the Dixboro Cougars' football season. Coach Tom Joyce had always made it plain that he'd not stand for squabbling on the squad. In case of a fight, he had warned, *both* the fighters would be thrown off the team—no matter who started it, or who threw the first punch.

So Win Hadley stood on the concrete locker-room floor below Dan Slade and fought a battle with himself. He stood there with his eyes fixed on Dan, unaware that the babble of voices had died down and that Archie and Matt and Red McGinley and the others had quietly formed a half circle around the two of them. It was now a battle of wills, and after a long, tense thirty seconds, the brittle silence was shattered by the sound of Dan Slade coughing nervously. He glanced quickly away from Win, and then, returning his gaze and seeing Win's expression unchanged, he jumped down from the bench, mumbling, "Oh, all right, if your skin's that thin—I'm sorry."

Dan pushed his way through the crowd and went to his locker. He dressed hurriedly in a simmering rage which at last came to the surface when he slammed his locker door shut with a vicious swing of his arm and all but ran from the building without even bothering to call to Archie Campbell to follow him.

But Archie did. Staring straight ahead, the big sandy-haired center went trotting obediently after his infuriated friend. In another minute, the roar of a motor starting and the squealing of rubber suggested that Dan Slade was leaving the scene of his humiliation as fast as his sport car would carry him.

Inside the locker room, Matt Hughes was hugging Win Hadley with pleasure, exclaiming, "Nice going, Win—you really took that stuck-up smart aleck down a peg. But I would have liked it better if you had let him have it!"

"Uh—uh," Win said, shaking his head. You'd be looking around for a new quarterback and right halfback."

"Maybe so," Charley Bantam put in. "But it'd almost be worth it."

"And of all people to talk about ball-hogging," Red McGinley added. "Why," he said, turning indignant, "that Dan Slade invented it!"

Win grinned at the look of outrage on Red's freckled face and got to his feet.

"Well," he said, "he apologized, so that's that. As far as I'm concerned, I've forgotten all about it."

Matt Hughes looked at Win and shook his head slowly.

"You may have forgotten it, Win," he said. "But I'll bet you all the tea in China that Dan hasn't."

CHAPTER FIVE

A Jealous Plotter

DAN DID NOT FORGET. Even if he had wanted to, such good intentions would have been defeated by the story which appeared in the *Crawford Record* on the following Saturday. Little George Slocum had outdone himself in his first piece accepted by the *Record,* a county newspaper which circulated throughout the towns in the Western Massachusetts Scholastic League. The article read:

NEW STAR SHINES
AT DIXBORO HIGH

* * * *

Young Hadley Shapes Up As
Cougar All-Time Great

By George (Scoop) Slocum

Who says lightning doesn't strike twice in the same place?

If Dixboro High School Athletic Field is any proof, then that old proverb got itself shattered and pretty beat up in general yesterday afternoon, as another Cougar great by the name of Hadley ran and passed the Dixboro Varsity to a 42–0 trouncing of a better-than-average Scrub team.

For the information of all you W.M.S.L. old-timers, the name of this Hadley happens to be Winfield, not Walter. And if Coach Tom Joyce himself is any judge, this Hadley is an even faster streak of greased lightning than his famous brother, Walter, who was in the habit of burning up local gridirons some eight years ago.

In yesterday's victory, Win Hadley had a hand in all but one of the six touchdowns scored during a slaughter that would have been bloodier had not Coach Joyce called a merciful halt. Not only did he pass twice to end Al Jacobson for touchdowns, but he lugged the leather over the last chalk stripe himself no less than three times. To top it off, he kicked six extra points—to say nothing of the way he directed the dazzling new Cougar offensive which Coach Joyce is primed to spring on his W.M.S.L. opponents this season.

There had been more, much more, all in little George's jaunty, bubbly style. But, unfortunately for some of those who read the *Crawford Record* in Dixboro that morning, and fortunately for others, the School Sports Editor who handled Scoop Slocum's copy had been forced to cut it by two-thirds. There just hadn't been room for any more.

For Dan Slade, this had been unfortunate. The paragraph which had mentioned Dan's splendid 46-yard scamper had landed in the wastebasket. And when Dan came down for breakfast, his father looked up from his paper with a puzzled expression.

"Say, son," he said, "I thought you told me you ran for a touchdown yesterday and had generally played a good game?"

"I did," Dan said, reaching for the paper.

He read Scoop's story, and as he did, his face turned red and white by turns—red with embarrassment and white with the fury of jealousy.

Owen Slade was watching his only son intently. When at last Dan had mastered his feelings and returned the newspaper, his father said, "Well?"

"Didn't you notice, Dad? That stupid Scoop Slocum didn't mention who scored the first touchdown. He was so busy flattering the great Win Hadley that he forgot who made the longest run of the game!"

"Now, now, son—take it easy."

"Well, it was! I was the star!"

Owen Slade stroked his chin reflectively.

"Seems to me, Dan, that Hadley boy didn't play a bad game, either."

This was more than Dan could bear. He got slowly to his feet. "I—I don't think I want any breakfast, Dad," he said, and then, to his father's amazement, he ran from the room.

For Win Hadley, it was perhaps fortunate that considerably more of George Slocum's praises never saw print. Otherwise, he would never have been able to stand the good-natured ribbing he received from his brother.

"Well, well, well," Walter said, laughing, as Win came into the kitchen and sat down opposite him. "It says here in the *Record* that a star is born."

"Oh?" Win said, lifting a thick slice of crumb cake from the plateful of buns on the table. "Have they named it yet?"

Walter grinned. "It says here the name is Hadley."

Win almost choked on his first mouthful of the delicious powdery cake.

"Wha-a-at?"

Still grinning, Walter said, "Here, let me read it for you." Then, in a syrupy voice, he began to ladle out Scoop Slocum's sweet talk, while his younger brother sat at the breakfast table with burning ears and crimson face. Once, he paused to ask, slyly,

"How much did you pay this Slocum boy, Win?"

"Aw, cut it out, Walt. Why don't you stick to the financial section and let me have the sports page? I don't believe it's there. I'll bet you're making it up."

"Thanks for the compliment. No, I'm not the writer your pal is. But just for proof, here it is." He shoved the paper across the table.

Win read rapidly, blushing more furiously than before. But when he came to the end of the article, he groaned and clapped his hand against his forehead.

"Oh, that crazy Scoop! He didn't even mention Dan!"

"So?"

"But things are bad enough already. This story will make Dan Slade hate me twice as hard!"

Then Win gave out an even louder moan and closed his eyes.

"And he let the cat out of the bag! Wait till Coach Joyce sees that line about "dazzling new Cougar offensive!"

Coach Joyce had seen it. Even as his star quarterback was moaning and groaning, an angry Tom Joyce was on the telephone laying down the law to George Slocum.

"And furthermore," he was saying, "you are not

to file any more stories on the team without first showing them to me."

"But, Coach," Scoop wailed, undaunted by the torrent of rebuke which had just been flowing his way. "But, Coach—that's censorship! That's violating the freedom of the press!"

Angry as he was, Tom Joyce could not repress a smile of amusement at Scoop's habit of using big words and big ideas.

"It is, eh? What about violations of the freedom of the student?"

"Whu-what?"

"Just what I said, young man. You'd better get these things in order right now. You've got to make up your mind which comes first, your school or your paper."

"But, Coach, they aren't in conflict."

"They're not, eh? Well, if you come down to football practice as a Dixboro High School student, loyal to his team, you'll be allowed in. But if you come down as a *Crawford Record* reporter, eager to tell all my secrets to the world, then you won't get in."

"Gee, Coach, if you put it that way . . ."

"It's the only way. Why, son, I'd never have let you within a mile of that field if I'd thought you were going to write a story about my new offensive. Put it this way—if you were a reporter and your country was at war, would you feel it was a violation of the freedom of the press if the government asked you not to write stories about war secrets?"

"Well, gee, it would be, in a way."

"Right, but in the interests of a higher loyalty—the security of your country. Understand?"

There was a long silence before Scoop said in a chastened voice, "Gee, Coach, I'm sorry."

"Not at all, boy. Just remember, now, to get these things in the right order."

Smiling again, happy to have made an important point of principle with a growing boy, Coach Tom Joyce hung up.

And when Scoop Slocum met the gang down at the Malt Shop that afternoon, and dolefully recounted the telephone conversation to a chuckling audience, he finished up with a droll shake of his head.

"Boy," he said, "when I read my story this morning and saw what the editor had done to it, I was mad enough to eat my press card. But, now, after hearing Coach Joyce, I could run out and buy him a new pair of scissors."

There was another shout of laughter, subsiding only when Win Hadley raised a hand and said, "I agree with you, Scoop—except for one thing."

"What's that?" Scoop asked, his sharp, inquisitive face all eagerness again.

"The fact that the editor cut out the part about Dan's touchdown."

Scoop shrugged. "I know what you mean, Win. But it couldn't be helped."

"Try telling that to Dan," Matt Hughes cut in. "I'll bet he hasn't cooled off yet."

As a matter of fact, Dan Slade hadn't.

Even as most of the members of the Dixboro Varsity were talking in the Malt Shop, discussing the coming opener with the Bedloe High Bulldogs, Dan Slade was busily hatching a scheme that would get him "even" with Win Hadley.

He and Archie Campbell had just entered the Campus Corner, a dimly lighted tavern on the outskirts of town, which was frequented by the students at Holden College and a number of the wilder boys from Farley Prep.

"C'mon, Arch, let's have a beer," Dan Slade said as they sat at a corner table.

"Er, if it's just the same to you, Dan, I'll take a birch beer."

"Birch beer! Are you kidding?"

Big Archie looked around him nervously.

"Er, no, Dan—but I don't want to do anything to make Coach Joyce mad at me."

"C'mon, don't be chicken! Have a beer. Besides, it's Saturday—and that means we get a day off from training rules, too."

Against his will, and because he had gradually

come under the rich boy's spell during the past few weeks, poor Archie Campbell consented. He drank slowly from his glass of beer while Dan Slade began talking fiercely.

"You know, Arch, I'm not going to be pushed around any more by that wise Win Hadley and his mob." He bristled angrily. "Did you see this morning's *Record*?" Archie nodded and Dan rushed on, sneering: " 'A new star shines at Dixboro High!' What boloney! I wonder how much Hadley paid that Slocum snoop to put that in?"

Archie didn't answer. He merely gulped down the last of his beer.

"Have another," Dan said, carelessly. "I'll take care of the check."

Archie nodded. He had gotten over his early embarrassment at accepting free rides and treats from Dan.

"Do you think it's fair for Hadley to get all the glory?" Dan burst out, and Archie shook his head slowly. He thought he was shaking it vigorously, but he was unaware that the beer had already muddled his reflexes.

"Of course it isn't," Dan went on. "I should get at least half of it. After all, I'm the fastest man on the squad." He glanced at Archie. Seeing the vacant look on his face, he smiled to himself and leaned toward him. "You want to help your old friend?" Archie nodded stupidly. "Well, here it is.

Without you in the center of the line, Archie, Win Hadley can't do anything. Oh, I know, that big boob of a Matt Hughes has something to do with it, but what I mean is it's you who keeps the center of the line solid. So who gets all the credit? Win Hadley!"

Archie Campbell blinked. A look of dull anger came over his rugged features.

" 'S right, Dan," he muttered.

"And look what he does to me," Dan rushed on bitterly. "He never lets me have the ball except when he knows I'm going to get smothered. Why, if I had you going downfield all the time, Arch, instead of protecting Hadley, I'd be getting away for long gains most of the time." Archie blinked again and Dan smiled slyly. "To say nothing of all the glory you'd get, Arch. You know, yourself, when you block a man at the line of scrimmage, nobody sees it. But when you block 'em out in the open, everybody does!" Dan winked. "It sure would help you get a scholarship, Arch."

For a moment, Archie Campbell seemed convinced. The word "scholarship" was an important one in his life, and his eyes glinted when he heard it. Then, suddenly, his brain cleared. He looked at Dan Slade in horror. He pushed his glass away and got to his feet.

"I'm getting out of here," he mumbled, and started for the door.

Dan Slade threw some money on the table and dashed after him.

"You know, Hadley needs a scholarship, too," he said smoothly. "Just like you, Arch. Are you going to give up your own career for Win Hadley's?"

Archie shouldered Dan aside. "Leave me alone," he snapped.

Dan Slade was stung. "Oh, yes? Funny you never told me to leave you alone when you needed a ride or a hamburger or a free movie." His voice turned nasty. "How much would you say you owed me by this time, Arch?"

Archie Campbell's face was red with embarrassment.

"So that's why you were so generous," he muttered.

"Maybe yes, maybe no. Depends on whether Archie Campbell keeps on being a stooge for Win Hadley or—"

"Or stooges for Dan Slade and gets paid for it," Archie cut in bitterly. "Listen, Dan," he went on, trembling from the distasteful business of speaking harshly to another person, "I'm going to pay you back what I owe you if I have to work nights all winter." He drew his breath and turned to face his tormentor. "And you'd better be playing for keeps when we play Bedloe next Saturday, or else the whole town will know about what you said to me tonight."

"Big deal!" Dan sneered. "As though you could tell them all."

"I won't have to. I'll just tell Scoop Slocum."

With that, Archie Campbell turned around and began walking back to town. Behind him, he heard Dan's sport car start and roar off in the opposite direction.

Funny, Archie Campbell said to himself as he trudged along, for the first time since football practice started, I feel pretty good.

CHAPTER SIX

Dan's Grandstand Play

It was a perfect day to open the football season.

The air was bright with the light of a gentle autumn sun. The sky above was blue, with here and there a candy tuft of white cloud, and in the woods that stood upon the slopes surrounding the Dixboro High athletic field were the brilliant reds and yellows of the dying leaves. There was a tang in the air, too, and that made it just right for playing football.

The captain of the Bedloe Bulldogs had won the toss and elected to receive. Now, he and his teammates were taking the field, resplendent in white jerseys shoulder-slashed with stripes of green, dark green silk pants and black helmets.

On the side lines, Coach Tom Joyce was talking to his boys in their black jerseys, gold pants and gold helmets.

"Remember, they're heavier—but that means nothing if you've got speed and guts. Hit 'em hard! Make sure they go down when you hit 'em. And you, Win, I want you to keep the keeper play under wraps for a while. Feel out the other team's defenses before you try it. Of course, if they go out in front, anything goes. Now, go out there and win!"

With sharp, yelping cries, the Dixboro Cougars streamed onto the field, and a roar of delight went up from the home-town crowd gathered in the wooden stands.

"Go get 'em, Dixboro," the shouts began.

"Chew 'em, Cougars!"

"Let's get that League title back where it belongs!"

Then came the silence before the kickoff.

The referee's whistle blew.

Matt Hughes approached the ball on choppy, tiptoe strides, and then he swung his powerful right leg high.

Thud!

The game was on, the season had begun.

It was a high kick, but none too far. It was taken on the 15 by one of the Bedloe backs. Win Hadley was startled to see the ball-carrier race directly upfield, and then dart sharply over to his left. A left-side runner! Automatically making the adjustment, and cutting to his right, Win felt his heart sink. The runner was fast, very fast. A screen of blockers had formed around him at the 30, and now he was churning past the 35.

He was going for a touchdown!

Then, a great shout burst from the Dixboro stands as little Charley Bantam sneaked through the cordon of blockers and brought the ball-carrier down with a shoe-string tackle. But the ball was already midfield, and Bedloe had begun the game with a bang!

"Signals: one, two, three, hike!" the Bedloe quarterback called, and the Dixboro linemen charged as he moved his feet. But the Bulldogs had merely shifted out of the T into a single wing, formation right, and the referee's whistle sounded the sad news that the Cougars had been drawn offside.

First down, five to go, ball on the Dixboro 45!

"Let's go, let's go," Win called to his teammates through cupped hands. "Watch that shift there!"

Again it came, but this time the Cougars were on the alert. It was formation left, toward Charley Bantam, Ed Walsh and Red McGinley, who held down the right side of the line on defense. The ball went back to that fast left-side runner. Following three-man interference, he swept wide. Red McGinley fought hard but the blockers were too much for him. He went down. Gabby Windham went down too. The runner was gobbling up the yardage, and the Bedloe fans were shrieking before

Teddy Scholari met him squarely and brought him to the grass.

First down again, on the Cougar 27. An 18-yard gain!

The next play, the Bulldogs ran to the right with their fullback carrying up the middle. But Matt Hughes fought off the blockers, got one big hand on him and set him up for Archie Campbell barging in to make the tackle. A gain of two yards.

Formation left again. Warily, Win Hadley began inching over from his own far wingback position. Again the snap went to the speedy halfback. He took a step back, faked a pass, collected his interference and split the tackle. The Bedloe blockers ran right over Ed Walsh and Charley Bantam. The runner gave Gabby Windham a limp leg, shook him off and dug his cleats into the turf for the breakaway stride. That was when Win Hadley hit him from the side. But he still had momentum and drove forward another four yards before he was downed. An 11-yarder, first down again—on the Cougar 14!

"Time!" Win Hadley called desperately to the referee. "Time out, please!"

The ref blew his whistle, pointed toward the Cougars and shouted: "Time out Dixboro!"

As Win Hadley gathered his bewildered teammates about him, there was a heavy silence in the home-town stands, broken only by the sound of a man shouting, "Come on, Dixboro, let's play football!"

"Wake up, fellows," Win pleaded as they knelt in a circle at the Dixboro goal line. "You're letting those blockers bowl you over."

"They hit pretty hard," Gabby Windham muttered, and Win turned on him fiercely. "They didn't stop little Charley, there. And you weigh fifteen pounds more than he does." He turned back to the rest of them. "Listen, they've got a left-side offense. The only time they tried the right, Matt and Archie stopped them. So Matt, you change places with Ed Walsh, and Archie, you move over to Gabby's spot. That ought to stop them," he said grimly, as the whistle blew again and they lined up on the 14.

Sure enough, formation left again. The ball went back to the speedster. But this time, Matt Hughes was charging with Archie Campbell shooting the gap behind him. The Cougar secondaries were closing in, too, and it appeared that the speedster circling lazily left was going to be nailed for a big loss.

Then, to Win's dismay, the tailback stopped, faced right and threw a perfect diagonal pass to his right end, standing all alone on the 5! The end gathered it in and just trotted over the goal line, to the delighted screams of the Bedloe rooting section and the shocked silence of the Dixboro stands.

The Bedloe play-caller had not only completely fooled Win Hadley, he had sent his pass receiver into Win's own territory!

Win looked despairingly at the bench. He felt worse when he saw Coach Tom Joyce shaking his gray head sadly, and he felt even worse than that when Dan Slade passed him and sneered, "Some strategy."

To make matters as bad as possible, Bedloe kicked the extra point.

The green-clad Bulldogs raced up the field chattering gleefully. They were seven points ahead, and the game was not yet two minutes old!

Suddenly, the loyal Dixboro rooting section came to life. As Win stood on the field, gritting his teeth and longing to get his hands on the ball, he heard the Cougar band break into the Dixboro High School Victory March, and then the cheerleaders were leading the crowd in the Cougar Fight Chant.

> Come on, Cougars!
> Come on, Cougars!
> Chew 'em up, chew 'em up—
> Fight, fight, fight!

In an instant, the old fire and determination came back to the team. Win Hadley felt all the tension go out of him and he could even swap grins with Dan Slade as the two youths stood in double safety within their own end zone.

The kickoff was a low one. It came angling down the left side lines, bouncing crazily before Teddy Scholari scooped it up, and giving the white-shirted Bulldogs plenty of time to swarm downfield. But Teddy gamely fought his way up to the Cougar 29. The crowd was on its feet as the chunky fullback bucked out of the arms of one tackler after another, finally going down under a snowstorm of white shirts. No sooner had the whistle blown than Teddy was on his feet, racing back to the huddle and shouting, "Let's go, gang! Those guys don't scare anybody!"

Grinning, Win slapped Teddy on the back as the team huddled.

"Nice going, Ted! Show 'em again, on a buck over right guard. Count of four."

The team broke and fairly sprinted for the line of scrimmage.

"Signals: one, two, three, four—"

Teddy Scholari came up fast, hugging the ball in close to his belly. But the Bedloe guard had charged the play and stopped the Dixboro fullback after a gain of only a yard. There was a groan from the Cougar stands.

But Win Hadley had seen something.

"They're charging," he said in the huddle. Let's try the draw, hey, Ted? We'll trap him."

Quickly, Win barked the signals. As he had hoped, the Bedloe guard was bracing for a charge. If only he would come in fast . . .

Win had the ball and was fading back, as though to pass. But as he ran past Teddy, crouching as though to give him protection, he slipped the ball off to him. Still pretending he had it, Win kept on fading. Teddy delayed a full second. The Bedloe guard charged. Gabby and Dan mouse-trapped him neatly, and Teddy went shooting through the gap the guard had left behind him. He rambled for eleven yards and a first down. The Cougar stands roared happily. At last, their team was moving!

On the next play, Win crossed the Bulldogs up. No sooner had the Cougars reached the line of scrimmage, than Archie hiked the ball to him. It took the enemy defenses by surprise, and they were powerless to move as Win jumped gracefully into the air and hit Al Jacobson legging it into the Bulldog secondary. By the time they dragged lanky Al to the earth, he had reached the Bedloe 41.

First down again, and in Bulldog territory!

The situation was ideal for the keeper. Win's eyes strayed to the bench. Coach Joyce carefully looked away. Other coaches might be guilty of coaching from the side lines, but not Tom Joyce.

Win made his decision.

"Keeper right. On five."

On the count of one, Dan Slade jogged into motion to the right. At four, Dan turned in and picked up speed. Win had seen him from the corner of his eye. As the ball hit his hands he quickly shoveled it out to Dan on a long, low spiral. It was a difficult play to attempt, but it worked as Dan stooped low to catch the ball and drove around the end. He might have gone all the way had he not gone slightly off balance in reaching for the pass. As it was he stumbled just inches short of a first down.

"Nice run, Dan," Win called gleefully as they huddled again. "We've got them on the run now. Keeper again, right. Al go deep, way, way down. Archie—give me plenty of cover. I'm going to try a long one. They'll be expecting us to pick up the easy first down. On three."

They ran back and lined up.

Win took the ball, faked off to Teddy charging up the middle, started right at an easy pace as though looking for a hole—and then, seeing Al Jacobson going down and in, he scampered quickly back to pass. Archie and Matt were covering beautifully, but one of the Bulldog linebackers had rushed into the Cougar backfield. He was bearing down on Win. Win straight-armed him, but the man came again. Win ran to the right, and now he could see Al Jacobson had turned it on and gotten behind the Bulldog safety.

Win Hadley stopped short, drew his arm back and let it go.

There was a great roar of excitement from the crowd, as the fans, too, saw that Al had outdistanced the safety man. And then the Dixboro stands went wild with delight as the fast-stepping end took the pass over his shoulder on the three and was over the goal in a single stride.

Win Hadley had thrown a 30-yard strike!

Even Dan Slade was grinning and pounding his hands like the rest of the overjoyed Cougars after Mat Hughes had plunked the ball squarely between the goal posts with what Scoop Slocum called "the most educated toe in western Massachusetts scholastic circles."

All tied up, now, at 7–7—and now it was the Bedloe stands that were wrapped in gloom.

And this time, the black-and-gold-caped Dixboro bandsmen really tootled away at their Victory March with a vengeance.

There wasn't any fancy return of Matt Hughes's kickoff, either, as there had been before. That was because the big tackle had booted the ball all the way down to the goal line, where the Bedloe quarter gathered it in and ran into a solid wall of tacklers on his own 17.

Once again, Bedloe shifted from the T into that bruising single wing. They had the power and they were going to use it. Obviously, the Bedloe coach hoped to wear down the lighter Cougars. Again and again, the Bedloe quarter shot those power plays at the Dixboro right side, hoping to roll over the defenders so as to spring that fleet-footed tail-back into open air. But Matt and Al Jacobson, with Archie Campbell behind them, and behind him, the chunky Teddy Scholari, gradually became a match for them.

At first, the Bulldogs rolled to another first down. They bit off solid chunks of five and six yards. Then they got another, but it took them three downs to make it. The Cougar defense was tightening up. Then, after Matt diagnosed a play and broke through to spill the tailback for a six-yard loss, the Bulldogs went to the air.

It was a buttonhook, from the tailback to his right end. The right end tore into Win Hadley's territory, then suddenly hooked around to come to a dead stop. It was a well-executed play, almost impossible to stop. Win Hadley chose the only way of breaking it up. The moment the end's hands touched the ball, Win slammed into him with a bone-jarring tackle. The ball spurted out of his hands for an incomplete forward pass.

Win got to his feet, vaguely conscious of the cheers in the stands. That tackle had shaken him up a bit, too. But he was over it in a second—rush-ing up to help Ed Walsh make the stop as the tricky Bedloe quarter tried to run the ball himself on a cross buck to his right.

Now, he had to kick.

And it was a beauty!

Win Hadley's respect for the Bedloe tailback grew even greater as he saw that ball leave his foot in a towering spiral. For a moment, he feared it would sail over Dan Slade's head, but the speedy Dan had taken off at the sound of shoe meeting leather. He had to race all the way back to his own 20 to keep ahead of it. But he got it, taking it over his shoulder on the dead run in a very pretty picture-play. And in the next instant, Dan was in trouble.

He was flying by the time he caught the ball and he kept on going backward in an attempt to outspeed the Bedloe ends closing in on him from either side. He went all the way back to his own 5, before making his turn upfield. On the bench, Jocko Williams groaned aloud and closed his eyes. Coach Joyce gritted his teeth, but emitted no sound.

The Bedloe left end had a clear shot at Dan now. At the least, he would spill him on the 2 or 3. At the worst, he would nail him behind the goal for a safety. As he left his feet, Dan Slade braked to an unbelievably sudden halt, spun around, teetered off-balance for a moment, and then recovered and started upfield to his left.

It was a marvelous display of muscular co-or-dination. He had reversed his field with such speed that half of the Bedloe boys had been thrown to the ground in an effort to make their own adjust-ment. Now, Win Hadley cut to the left, too, shout-ing at his teammates to form a blocking screen. They did. They mowed the bewildered Bedloe boys down like wheat, and Dan Slade came gallop-ing up to the 30, the 40, midfield, the Bedloe 45, the 40—and there, the tailback burst through the interference with a desperation lunge and cross-blocked Dan out of bounds at the 36.

By the time Dan Slade had reached his own 40 yard line, everyone within the athletic field—in-cluding the coaches—had come to his feet with an excited yell. By the time he had been knocked out of bounds, the field had all but rocked to the deaf-ening shouts from both stands, and even as the referee began pacing the ball inbounds to resume play, the babble of voices continued.

"Boy," Coach Joyce said, as he at last returned to his seat and the noise began to subside, "I don't want to have to look at many more of those."

Jocko grinned, "That's why coaches get gray, eh, Tom?"

"Well, it turned out all right—so it's all right. But, boy! Going backward for running room cer-tainly isn't my idea of the right way to return a punt. That's just grandstanding."

CHAPTER SEVEN

Beat Those Bulldogs!

IN THE HUDDLE, Dan Slade was grinning happily. The roar of the crowd in his ears was the sound Dan Slade loved best.

Win Hadley eyed him soberly.

"Winded?"

Dan shook his head.

"Feel like carrying again? They won't be looking for you."

Dan's head bobbed eagerly. This was just to his taste, and he strove to conceal the fact that he really was winded from that long backward-and-forward sprint.

"Good," Win said. "Go real wide this time. I'll try to draw them in before I flip out to you. On six."

The team lined up. Win fairly drawled the signals, hoping to give Dan plenty of time as he went loping into motion on the first number. Archie hiked it to him. Win ran to his right. As he had expected, the Bedloe end wasn't paying too much attention to Dan. The fleet Cougar back already had him by a step. Win made as though to lunge off tackle, drawing the end toward him. Then he flipped to Dan. He led Dan by a full stride, and it was a perfect toss—perfect, that is, as long as Win could figure Dan for his usual quick burst of speed. But too many hours at the Campus Corner had softened Dan and he was gasping for breath as he dived desperately for the ball. It just hit his finger tips and rolled free.

"Fumble!" the Bedloe players roared with one voice.

There was a wild scramble. Fully a half dozen boys had their hands on the pigskin but couldn't trap it. At last, there was a confused pile-up, and after the referee had pulled the boys to their feet, one by one, he turned and swung an emphatic arm in the direction of the Dixboro goal.

Bedloe had recovered!

As the Bulldog cheering section roared its approval, an angry murmur ran through the Dixboro stands.

"Watch where yer throwing it, Hadley!" a man shouted.

"Yeah," shrilled another. "You're not playing basketball out there, you know."

Win heard the taunts, and flushed angrily. It hadn't been his fault. Hadn't he asked Dan if he was winded? Win glanced anxiously at the bench. What he saw reassured him. Coach Tom Joyce had his eyes on Dan Slade, and as he studied him, there was a worried frown on his forehead. He knows, Win thought, relieved. You can't put much over on Coach Joyce!

Now the teams had changed goals, and Bedloe was starting the second quarter with the straight single wing, sometimes shifting into a double wing. They had given up the pretense of lining up in the T and were trying harder than ever to grind Dixboro down. But they got nowhere and had to kick. Dixboro couldn't move, either—and the second quarter was turned into a kicking duel.

Again and again, Win Hadley and Bedloe's star tailback exchanged booming punts, each trying to pin the other team back into the coffin corner where a fumble might mean the break that would spell touchdown. But both kickers were evenly matched, and they lifted their punts so high in the air that their ends had plenty of time to get downfield and nail the safety men in their tracks. In fact, as the quarter wore on, both Dan Slade and the Bulldog safety took to signaling for fair catches.

Then, the football fortunes seemed to favor Dixboro. Win got off a low twisting punt from his own 39. He groaned as he felt the ball slide off the side of his foot. A bad kick, he thought at first. But it was a good one. It rolled away from the scuttling Bedloe safety and bounced deeper and deeper into Bulldog territory. When it finally rolled dead on the Bedloe 6, Win was overjoyed.

"All right, let's go get 'em!" he shouted. "Hit 'em hard and make 'em fumble."

The Bedloe stands were silent as their heroes lined up in the shadow of their own goal posts. Could they blast through the stiffening Dixboro defenses and get out of the danger zone? It didn't look like it. The Cougars were in a seven-man line, with the secondary in close. They were going to pack the line of scrimmage.

Win Hadley had a sudden premonition, and he turned to yell at Dan Slade.

But it was too late.

The Bulldog tailback took two short backward steps as he received the pass from center, and then swung his leg in a quick kick.

The ball sped like a shot over the head of Dan Slade. He had been caught flat-footed, as had the whole Dixboro forward wall. Dan wheeled and raced after the ball. He overtook it on his own 41, turned and ran laterally across the field in another attempt to outspeed the converging Bedloe tacklers. But the important element of surprise had been all with the Bulldogs and Dan never had a chance. He went down under a blizzard of white jerseys.

Once again, the gibes rose from the crowd. Irritated at having seen Bedloe turn the tables so quickly, some of the more hotheaded among the Dixboro followers were shouting their disapproval.

"Hey, Hadley, you big bonehead," one of them jeered. "Haven't you ever heard of a quick kick before? Some captain," he sneered, and opened his mouth to yell another insult. But, unfortunately for him, he had chosen the wrong place in the stands to display his bad manners. A strong hand closed around his shoulder and he turned around to gaze into the set, white face of Walter Hadley.

"That boy happens to be my brother," Walt said evenly. "And if I hear you say one more word about him, I'll take you under the stands and teach you some manners! Now keep quiet and leave the boys alone."

Shamefaced, the man mumbled his apologies and turned back to watch the game.

But Win Hadley hadn't heard. He had been watching how painfully Dan Slade got to his feet after the Bulldogs unpiled, and how slowly he walked over to the huddle. Coach Tom Joyce had seen it too, and was on his feet in an instant.

"Okulski, go in for Slade," he called to a husky youth in the middle of the bench. The boy almost tripped as he leaped to his feet, seized his helmet and ran onto the field. Win's heart sank as the youth came on the field.

Emil Okulski was a power runner. Though he was fairly fast, he couldn't match Dan's speed. Besides, he was only a sophomore—and this would be his first Varsity high school game. For a moment, as he watched Dan jog slowly from the field, Win felt a rush of anger. If only Dan would stay in condition like everybody else!

But then he had a sudden idea, and he turned quickly to Gabby Windham in the huddle.

"Gabby, let's try the keeper left!"

Gabby gaped in astonishment.

"Me?"

"Why not? You know how it's done. And it's simple enough. They'll be looking for us to keep on hitting the right side, anyway. It's our only chance with Dan out. C'mon—let's try it! On five."

They broke out of the huddle and lined up, and as they did, the Bedloe linemen began to taunt them.

"My, my, is this the Dixboro 40-yard line?"

"Dearie me, how did such a terrible thing ever happen?"

Win could feel the growl rumbling in Archie Campbell's chest as he laid a hand on Archie's back and surveyed the field. Then he, too, crouched—took the ball and was dashing left. He drew his right knee high in the air, as though he were leap-ing to flip to Gabby on the flank, then lowered his head and powered through a narrow hole between tackle and guard.

He felt the Bedloe tackle's hands clutching at his waist as he streaked by, but he shook him off. Now he was in their secondary. The wingback was driving up to stop him. Win slowed, cut to his right, shifted the ball into his right arm and drove a straight-arm straight into his face. Now he was running diagonally across the field with open coun-try ahead of him. He had crossed the midfield stripe and was plunging into Bulldog territory when the fleet tailback came tearing up from his safety position and ran him out of bounds on the Bedloe 24.

It had been an electrifying, broken-field run of thirty-five yards through practically the entire Bed-loe secondary, and now the Cougars of Dixboro High were on the move again!

Quickly huddling his players so as not to lose any momentum, Win Hadley barked, "Buck to Emil, inside tackle," and they raced up to the line of scrimmage. Win felt the smooth co-ordination of the line as he whirled and handed off to the young halfback. Emil Okulski cuddled the ball in both hands and barreled ahead to the Bedloe 19. The Cougars had caught fire!

The cheerleaders were chanting, "We want a

touchdown. We want a touchdown!" as the team lined up again and Gabby Windham knifed down to the 11 on his favorite dive play. Then it was the keeper left with Win lateraling to Gabby for four more; and on the next play, Win kept the ball himself—slicing inside the tackle, reversing his field and traveling the remaining seven yards to the end zone without a hand laid on him!

"Yeah, Hadley. Yeah, Hadley. Hadley, rah, rah!" the cheerleaders were shouting, when they weren't turning delirious somersaults.

But as Win came running out of the end zone, he made a point of pounding little Charley Bantam on the back. For it had been Charley who had thrown himself at the Bedloe linebacker at the precise moment when Win cut to his right, thus clearing the path to pay dirt for him.

Then Win was kneeling on the gridiron, taking Archie's perfect pass from center, plunking it on the ground and holding it there as Matt Hughes swung his leg and made the score: Dixboro 14, Bedloe 7.

And in another minute, after Bedloe had received the kickoff and thrown a pair of desperation passes, the half ended with the score that way.

In the second half, the rejuvenated Cougars ran away from their heavier but slower opponents. Bedloe just never seemed able to recover the drive they had shown in the opening minutes of the game, and as the minutes passed by, their big forwards seemed to get slower and slower as the fast-charging Dixboro linemen boxed them, trapped them and generally ran them into the ground.

Win Hadley had never played football before as he played in that second half. Time after time he brought the crowd to its feet as he ran that keeper play with a deft daring that was the despair of the Bedloe coach. On any given play it was impossible to guess what Win was going to do. He never made his move until the last second, and when he unlimbered his throwing arm midway in the third period and began hitting Al Jacobson and Teddy Scholari with buttonhooks, down-and-outers or the stop-and-go, it turned out to be too much for the demoralized Bulldogs. They simply collapsed.

Dan Slade was back for the second-half onslaught, too, though it was a greatly chastened Dan Slade.

During the intermission, Coach Joyce had drawn him aside and with a few short, sharp words had told him that he would either get back in condition or turn in his uniform. So Dan cut out the fancy stuff and turned in a steady game that included a fifteen-yard dash around right end for a touchdown.

But his performance was not up to Win Hadley's. Win scored the final touchdown, picking off a Bedloe desperation pass in the last quarter and returning it twenty-five yards for a touchdown. Before that, his thread-the-needle passes to Al Jacobson had set up the fourth score, a quick pop by Teddy Scholari from the 4.

Since one of Matt Hughes's try for point was blocked, the final score was 34 to 7. It might have been higher, had not Coach Tom Joyce cleared the bench of substitutes right after Win's touchdown interception. Coach Joyce was never a man to run up a score.

When the team came running off, the roar that went up for Win Hadley made it plain to an infuriated Dan Slade that the crowd had forgotten all about his thrilling punt return early in the game. Dan came off the field grinding his teeth and, when the game ended, he turned away from his whooping teammates as they gathered around Win and slapped him on the back. He dawdled behind as they ran from the field to the locker room, and when he saw his chance, he sneaked off and made for his sport car parked outside the gate.

He got in and drove home, angrily honking his horn at the Dixboro High students and bandsmen as they snake-danced through the streets to the tune of the Dixboro Victory March.

"Darn fools," he muttered under his breath. "I suppose they think they're going to win the League." He snorted. "Well, they won't be dancing in the streets when they hear Dan Slade's quit the team. No coach is going to talk to me like that! And they can have their goody-goody ball-hog of a Win Hadley. See how far they get with him!"

CHAPTER EIGHT

Walt's Big Deal

THE VICTORY CELEBRATION was still in progress as Win Hadley and Matt Hughes turned down Elm Street on their walk home from the athletic field. They could still hear the faint strains of the Victory March from the direction of Station Square.

Matt grinned happily.

"Boy, oh, boy—there's nothing like the football season, is there?"

"Uh, uh. I sure hope it's like this every Saturday night."

"It will be," Matt said confidently, shooting a glance full of admiration at his friend. "Just keep on playing like you did today, and we can't miss."

Win laughed. "Flattery," he said, pushing Matt into the hedge, "will get you nowhere."

"Mebbe so," Matt sputtered, climbing out of the hedge. "But I'd still like to try it." His handsome face puckered in a wry expression. "I can just see what Scoop will say in tomorrow's *Record*. 'Matt Hughes's educated toe accounted for the first of his four conversions.'" He grinned "Just one line. That's all I'll get. And I bet you get half a page!"

Win laughed.

"Trouble with you, Matt, you don't pay Scoop enough."

Matt sniffed. "His rates are too high. Only quarterbacks can afford them. Well, here's your house, old glory-hound. See you tonight?"

"Right. So long, Matt."

With practiced grace, Win Hadley sailed over the front hedge and went rattling up the porch stairs. He was still going fast when he entered the house, but when he got to the dining room he was so astonished he had to brake himself to a skidding halt.

There were candles on the dining table and the good silver and dishes were laid out on a snowy white linen tablecloth.

"Hey!" he shouted. "What's going on?"

Mrs. Hadley and Walter came into the room, both smiling slyly.

"Oh, come on, now," Win said. "Don't tell me you're going to all this fuss just because we happened to win a—"

Walter grinned and nudged Mrs. Hadley gently.

"Thinks he's the only star in the house, doesn't he, Mom?"

Mrs. Hadley smiled and winked at Win.

Flustered, Win looked back and forth from one to the other. He didn't know what to say. With another grin, Walter came over and slapped him on the back.

"The truth of the matter is that we *are* having a celebration, Win. Looks like both the Hadley boys did pretty well today. You with a football, me with a fountain pen."

"Fountain pen?"

"Well, not quite yet, Win. But it will come to that. The fact is, that deal I mentioned to you a few weeks ago is coming through."

"Walt! No kidding?"

"Honest! It looks like the Slade Sawmill Company will have a new fleet of cars in another month or so, and it looks like they'll be buying them from me!"

Win's mouth flew open.

"A whole *fleet* of cars, Walt? Oh, boy—that's terrific!"

Walter Hadley beamed. The family responsibility which had weighed so heavily on his young shoulders for the past few years seemed as light as a speck of dust now.

"Well, it *is* pretty good, Win," he said modestly.

"As a matter of fact, it's going to be the biggest deal in the agency's history."

Win's eyes went wide and he brushed his hand over his short dark hair excitedly. As his mother propelled him gently to his seat at the dining table, he could do nothing but shake his head and repeat, "Boy, is that terrific!" over and over again. His enthusiasm made his brother laugh.

Walt winked at Mrs. Hadley again, and asked, "What was the score today, Win?"

"Whu-what?"

Now, Mrs. Hadley had to laugh.

"My goodness, Winfield Hadley, I never thought I'd see the day you'd forget the score of a Dixboro High School football game. But now I've seen it."

Win grinned.

"Well, it *was* 34 to 7, now that you ask me, but I'll have to admit Walt had me rattled." He turned on his brother. "How did you swing it?"

"Oh, I just kept bothering Mr. Slade, I guess, until he had to give me the contract in self-defense." More seriously, he went on: "Actually, the Slade Company has been using outmoded autos for the past three or four years. Mr. Slade told me he hated to lay out all that money for today's high-priced cars, but when I showed him how much he was losing by hanging onto those old gas-eaters, he changed his mind." Walt smiled. "So he put in an order for six sales cars and six pickup trucks, for delivery by Thanksgiving."

Win shook his head and gazed at his older brother in admiration. His eyes shone and he started to say, "Boy—"

"—is that terrific!" Walt finished for him, and all three of them burst out laughing.

"Wait'll I tell Matt!" Win burst out, after the laughter had subsided, but Walter shook his head soberly.

"I don't think you'd better tell anyone, Win," he said. "I don't want this to leak out. Of course, Mr. Slade says he's given me his word that he'll order through me. But, still, someone else might hear of it and go hotfooting it over to the mill with a better offer. And business is business, Win; don't you ever forget that."

Dixboro High's star quarterback nodded gravely.

"Whatever you say, Walt. I won't tell a soul."

"Good. And, now, here comes Mom with a little surprise for us."

The kitchen door swung open and Mrs. Hadley appeared, bearing a huge platter containing the main dish. Win Hadley's eyes sparkled.

"Seven weeks until Thanksgiving, and we're having turkey already!"

Oddly enough, the Owen Slade family was having turkey too.

But the Slade gobbler was served by a maid in a black dress and white linen apron. It was bigger, naturally, though it didn't come up to Mrs. Hadley's tom in flavor. And, of course, it rested on a costly silver platter underneath a splendid crystal chandelier, surrounded by shining silver and glittering china and glassware.

"Say, this bird is really good," Mr. Slade said, looking down the long table at Mrs. Slade. He glanced at Dan, who had been silent throughout the meal. "What do you say, son—like it?"

"Not bad," Dan mumbled, and his father shot him a sharp glance.

"Say, what's bothering you, boy? You haven't said a word since we sat down to eat. Feeling ill?"

Dan shook his head.

"What's wrong, then? Confound it, you can't be feeling low after what your gang did to Bedloe this afternoon. Left 'em for dead, I'd say. And that was a mighty fine run you reeled off on that punt return."

Dan's face brightened and he looked up eagerly.

"Did you think so?"

"Certainly I did. Though I must say you were taking a big chance going back like that." Dan's face fell, and his father rushed on. "But you scored a touchdown, didn't you?" Dan nodded, glumly. His father looked at him in amazement. Then he said, "By the way—why did Coach Joyce take you out of the game after that quick kick? I thought you were going pretty good."

Dan Slade looked desperately down the table at his mother. She smiled at him fondly. He turned to his father.

"I, I got the wind knocked out of me," he said, assuring himself that it wasn't a complete lie.

"Oh. Well, you certainly had your wind back in the second half. You looked fine on that touchdown run." He turned to the maid. "Here, Netty, let me have some more of that delicious white meat."

Dan stared at his father miserably. He wondered if he dared tell him right here and now that he was quitting the team. He stole a glance at his mother. She'd back him up. She always did, and she had always been against football. Dan opened his mouth to speak, but then he heard his father say something that changed his mind.

"That Hadley boy, now," Owen Slade was saying. "He's really something. They say he's better than his brother." Mr. Slade smiled. "I doubt that very much. Why, I honestly believe that Walter Hadley could sell ice to the Eskimos."

"How do you mean, dear?" Mrs. Slade asked.

"Why, he's been after me for six months to trade in my old fleet and buy a new one. And darned if he didn't convince me he was right. Met him yesterday at Rotary and gave him the go-ahead."

"How nice for Mrs. Hadley," Mrs. Slade said. "She can't have been having a very easy time of it since the doctor died."

"That may be, dear. But it was young Hadley's business proposal, not his need, that convinced me. You don't go in for charity when you're in business, my dear."

Dan Slade struggled to conceal his elation. Why, the whole thing was just made to order! He had forgotten all about Win's family's circumstances. And, now, his brother was just about to make a business deal that must be very important to them. And with whom? Dan Slade's father!

"Say, Dad," Dan said casually. "How many cars would there be in a fleet?"

"Twelve. Not all cars, though, son. Half of them are trucks."

"Oh. Sounds like quite a bit of money."

"I should say so. Close to fifty thousand dollars, I'd say."

"Would—er—ah—would Win Hadley's brother make much out of that?"

"Oh, my, yes! Why, I'd reckon it at—" Mr. Slade stopped talking and gazed in surprise at his son. "Say, Dan, don't tell me you're taking an interest in the business at last!"

"Now, now, Owen," Mrs. Slade said tartly. "Don't start picking on our Danny again."

Dan Slade threw up a hand to cut his doting

mother short. He started to question his father again.

"When does the deal go through, Dad?"

"Well, the vehicles are for delivery by Thanksgiving. But the deal goes through as soon as Walter Hadley gets the contracts drawn up. A week or two, I'd say—depending on how soon we can iron out the details."

Dan smiled. He wasn't going to quit the Cougars, after all. In fact, he had never felt better about football in his life.

"You know, Dad," he said, "I think I'd like a little more of that white meat after all."

CHAPTER NINE

An Ultimatum

THE FIRST THING that Win Hadley did when he came downstairs on the Sunday after the Bedloe game was to fetch the *Crawford Record* from the front porch and turn to the School Sports Section. He saw the headline and groaned. It read:

HADLEY IS ONE-MAN TEAM AS
COUGARS CHEW BEDLOE, 34–7

"Oh, that crazy Scoop!" Win moaned aloud. "What will the others think when they see this?"

Win continued to read, fuming as he did so. It was another bouquet from Scoop's flowery pen, and Win Hadley was levelheaded enough to realize that it was actually poison ivy as far as harmony on the team was concerned.

He knew that for a fact the moment he entered

the Malt Shop that afternoon. His ears burned at the cries that greeted him.

"If it ain't Win Hadley himself! Well, well, to what do we owe this honor?"

"Why, there's only one of him. And all the time I thought there were eleven!"

One of the girl cheerleaders was seated at the counter having a Coke, and when she saw Win come in, she slid off her stool and turned and yelled to the rest of her friends: "Here's our dream—the one-man team!"

And, of course, Red McGinley had to puff up his cheeks like a tuba player and chant:

Oom-pah-pah. Oom—pah-pah.
Rah, rah, Hadley—rah, rah, rah!

If the ribbing was bad enough to take, the outright resentment of some of the fellows was even worse.

Al Jacobson tried not to show it, but Win could tell he wasn't any too happy about Scoop's story when he pointed out that the finest passer in the world needs someone to catch what he throws.

"You know, I did score the tying touchdown, Win," he added.

"You said it!" Gabby Windham put in heatedly. "And what about the way we broke the game open when we started to run the keeper to my side?"

He looked coldly at the team captain and quarter-back. "Seems to me you always manage to hog the limelight, Hadley."

"But I don't," Win began, desperately. "Listen, fellows, let's not act like this. It'll wreck the team. Honestly, you'd think *I* wrote that story. Can I help what Scoop puts in the paper?"

"He's right, Gabby," Teddy Scholari said, shooting Win a reassuring smile. "If you want to blame somebody, blame Slocum."

"Listen to them, Arch," a deep voice said, and they all turned to see Matt Hughes and Archie Campbell come in the door. "Just what you'd expect from the glory boys, isn't it? All the halfbacks and the ends squabbling about who scored what when." Matt put his hands on his hips and faced them all. "Listening to you guys, you'd never think there was such a thing as a tackle or a guard or a center." He grinned at Al Jacobson. "You paste your clippings in the scrapbook I gave you, yet?"

Archie Campbell snickered as Al grinned sheepishly and pretended to throw a punch at Matt's jaw, and in the next instant the ugly mood had vanished. But Win Hadley did not forget it and he became more than ever concerned when Archie drew him aside and began talking to him in low tones.

"If I were you, Win, I'd try to talk to Dan Slade," Archie said, averting his head so that Win could not see the shame in his eyes. "I mean, for the good of the team."

"I don't understand you, Arch."

"Listen," Archie went on, with patient doggedness, "you just saw how sore some of the guys are about the publicity you've been getting. Well, they're sweethearts of yours compared to Dan Slade." Archie looked gloomily at his feet and went on. "For a while, I was pals with Dan—and I know what he thinks. He hates the thought of playing second fiddle to anyone. He'd do anything to take the play away from you, Win, honest he would. Believe me, I know!"

"What do you know, Arch?"

The husky center's eyes went to the ceiling again.

"Never mind, I just do. I couldn't tell you—for the good of the team. But for the good of the team, Win, I think you'd better talk to Dan. We know we can't win the League without him. Why, that running to the left yesterday was just a fluke—and you know it." Win nodded as Archie continued, "They were taken by surprise, and they never did get over it. But you read what Crawford did to Framton yesterday?"

Win Hadley rolled his eyes.

"I'll say I did! Forty-five to nothing."

"Yeah, and Framton was supposed to be much

better this year. Well, if we're going to beat Crawford, we're going to need Dan Slade's speed."

Win nodded, but then he frowned.

"Right, Arch—but what can I do?"

Archie Campbell flushed and shifted uneasily.

"You can butter him up, that's what. Oh, I
know, Win, it sounds pretty cheesy to put it that
way. I just mean you could make him feel that he's
important. That's the trouble with him, I know,
but if Dan Slade doesn't feel that he's the star—
then he doesn't want to play. And the trouble is,
we need him."

Win got to his feet. He regarded Archie Campbell with a new-found respect. He had never
thought the big center was quite that sharp.

"Thanks, Arch. I think you may have something. In fact, I'm going to take a walk over to
Dan's right now.

Archie grinned and held up crossed fingers.

"Here's hoping," he said, as Win Hadley turned
and quietly left the Malt Shop.

Dan Slade had just reread the *Crawford Record*
for the umpteenth time, when the front doorbell
rang. Vaguely, through the red mists of his anger,
he could hear Netty coming from the dining room
to answer it. He heard her questioning someone,
and then, to his astonishment, he heard Netty call

upstairs to him: "Dan, there's a young man named Win Hadley to see you."

Dan's first reaction was one of fury. He came to his feet with a growl, rolling the newspaper in his hand like a club. Then he smiled. Well, well, well, he thought to himself. Then, to Netty, he called, "Show him in the parlor, Netty."

Dan rubbed his hands. *Parlor* was right. *"Come into my parlor," said the spider to the fly*. It was too good to be true. Dan had succeeded in worming all the details about Walter Hadley's deal out of his father before Mr. and Mrs. Slade left the house to visit friends in Twining. He had been wondering just how to approach Win Hadley. And now, here was Win coming to him.

Smiling with false friendliness, Dan went into the parlor.

"Why, if it isn't Win Hadley! How are you, Win?"

"Er, fine, Dan."

"What brings you here?"

"Well—er—that is, have you read the *Record* yet?"

Dan turned to sit down, to prevent Win from seeing the look of hatred that flashed over his face. When he was seated, he glanced up and said, "Well, yes, I did skim through it. I see Scoop Slocum had a story on our game yesterday."

Now, it was Win Hadley's turn to be amazed.

"You mean you didn't notice how Scoop went—er—overboard in saying nice things about me?"

Dan waved an airy hand.

"Oh, that . . ."

"But, I thought—"

Dan Slade was obviously enjoying himself.

"Why, Win, who cares who gets the credit as long as we win? The team's the thing, Win—just as Coach Joyce says. Anyway," Dan added slyly, "I think Scoop will be writing me up a bit in the next few games."

"How's that, Dan?" Win asked, puzzled.

"Why, with you feeding me the ball the way you say you will, how can I miss?"

"But, Dan, you must be mistaken! When did I ever say that?"

Dan smiled and examined his fingernails.

"I sure hope your brother makes that deal with my father." There was a moment of silence, while Win forced his mind to adjust to this abrupt change of subject. Then, shaking his head mournfully, Dan continued, "I'd sure hate to see him lose out." Watching Win narrowly, Dan Slade leaned forward and patted him on the knee. "But, of course, he won't, you know. Not with his kid brother feeding the old apple to Owen Slade's son." He sat back and winked broadly at Win.

In an instant, Win had grasped what Dan Slade was driving at.

Rising from his chair, he leaned over to seize Dan by the front of his sweater and pull him half out of his seat.

"Stop beating around the bush, you dirty black-mailer!" he growled. "Spit it out. Tell me in plain words what you mean!"

Dan's reply was to shake himself free and gaze back up at Win with a nasty smile around his lips.

"I see the one-man team has got the message," he sneered.

Crack!

With a blur of speed, Win Hadley slammed the back of his hand across Dan Slade's face. Dan went white with rage.

"Go ahead, try it again with your fist," Dan snarled. "Then, you'll be sure to ruin yourself. We'll both get chucked off the football team, and then my father will tell Walt what he thinks of the Hadley manners!"

The color drained from Win Hadley's face. His heart seemed to be made of lead. He felt so desperate that he was on the verge of being physically ill. He glared at Dan and, through tight lips, said, "You *are* trying to blackmail me, aren't you?"

Dan shrugged. "It's your word."

"You're telling me that if I don't feed the ball to you, you'll wreck my brother's deal with your father."

Dan shrugged again. "You said it; I didn't."

Win Hadley turned as though he were leaving. "I'm going to see your father in the morning."

"Go ahead," Dan goaded him, his voice heavy with sarcasm. "I'm sure Dad would rather believe a stranger than his own son."

Win Hadley stood rooted to the spot. Then he swung slowly around to face Dan Slade.

"If I had your brains, Dan," he began, but the rich boy interrupted him with an irritable wave of his hand.

"Cut the soft soap, Hadley. I think we understand each other. See you at practice tomorrow."

With that, Dan got up and left the room. As he walked upstairs, he called to the maid to show Win out.

CHAPTER TEN

Ups and Downs

WIN HADLEY HARDLY SLEPT that night.

He tossed and turned so frequently in the unhappiness of his dilemma that his mother came into his room twice to ask him if he was ill.

The way Win saw it, there was no way out. If he maintained his loyalty to the school and ran the team without favoritism, he was liable to cause his family serious financial injury. If he did what Dan Slade wanted him to do, he would hurt the team. Win Hadley knew very well that the keeper play depended more on his judgment and timing than on Dan Slade's speed. Keep feeding the ball to Dan, and you'd no longer be able to keep the enemy guessing.

Then Win began to wonder just how Dan would be able to block Walter's deal. Certainly, he couldn't do it openly. Mr. Slade was too wise a businessman to allow his son to influence him for no good reason. Then, how? Secretly, of course; that was Dan Slade's way. A pity that such a fine mind should be so twisted. But, again—how? Win Hadley couldn't figure it out.

At last, he went to sleep with his mind made up on two points: first, the only honest course was to play the game the way he'd always played it; and, second, Dan Slade was bluffing. He would never dare interfere with his father's business.

But Win's resolve was badly shaken that afternoon as the squad dressed for practice. Dan came up to Win in the locker room and said, "How'd you like to take a ride to Framton with me tonight?"

"What for?" Win said mechanically, pulling on his football shoes.

"Oh, I think there's something wrong with the fuel pump in my car. Square Deal Motors where Dad bought it is in Framton." Dan smiled meaningfully. "Fellow who sold it to us is sure a crackerjack of a salesman. Yessir, he really loves to wheel 'em and deal 'em. You know what his slogan is, Win?"

Win Hadley looked up with a sinking heart. He half braced himself for what was coming next.

"He says, 'I will never be undersold.'"

Dan Slade winked and walked away to his own locker, leaving Win Hadley as miserable as he had been the day before. So that would be it! All Dan had to do was tip off the other auto agencies, and they'd be swarming around the sawmill plant like bees in clover. Win stood up. He no longer had the power even to be mad at Dan, he felt so washed-out. He saw good old open-faced Matt Hughes standing watching him, and he took a half-step toward him, as though he wanted to tell his friend the whole rotten story. But he pulled up short. He couldn't. For the moment, until he could get his mind straightened out, he couldn't do anything that might make Dan Slade go off half-cocked. He had to save Walter's deal! Yes, he thought grimly, and he had to play an honest game of football too.

With a deep groan of anguish that could be heard from one end of the locker room to the other, Win Hadley jumped to his feet and clattered over the cement floor and out the door. He tore out onto the field almost blinded by the tears of rage and frustration that sprang up in his eyes. Spying a loose football, he stooped, scooped it up and then kicked it on the run with a savage swing of his right leg. He fairly leaped into the ball, he was so overcome with emotion, and the pigskin took off downfield as though it had been fired from a launching pad.

"Did you see that?" Jocko Williams called to Coach Tom Joyce. "I'll bet that punt traveled sixty yards in the air if it traveled an inch!"

"I saw it," Coach Joyce said, more disturbed than pleased. "And I'm wondering what could have made the Hadley boy light into that ball so. He's not one to show his temper, you know, Jocko. Something must be wrong."

As the week's practice wore on, Coach Joyce discovered that something was really wrong. The Varsity backfield couldn't do anything right. Everyone but Teddy Scholari seemed to have two left feet, and Win Hadley was the worst offender.

He was overthrowing his passes because he was trying too hard. His hand-offs were sloppy and he couldn't have fooled a baby with his faking. When he ran the keeper he had none of his old decisiveness or daring. Frequently, he held onto the ball too long and was tackled dead in his tracks by Scrub linemen. Or else he flipped it too soon to Dan Slade and gave the play away. And when Win went to his left on the keeper, the results were worse. But, here, it was as much Gabby Windham's fault as Win's, for Gabby was still pouting over Scoop's story and was not too anxious to block for the quarterback when he decided to run the ball himself.

The only pleasure Coach Joyce could take from practice was the steady work of the center of the line. Ed Walsh and Matt Hughes at tackle, Charley Bantam and Bill Keller at the guards and Archie at center were getting better and better as a unit. Al Jacobson and Red McGinley at end were fine on defense, too, but Coach Joyce had noticed a certain carelessness in their manner of going out for passes.

All in all, as Coach Joyce confided to Jocko Williams on the Thursday night before the Framton game, things were "a sorry mess."

"I tell you, Jocko, I've a good mind to give 'em a day off tomorrow. I think they're stale."

"Stale! With only one game played so far? How could that be?"

The coach frowned and stroked his square jaw. "But they have no pep. They've lost their bounce."

"You mean Hadley has, Tom."

"Eh?"

"Now, come on, Tom—you know Hadley's our key man. He's the team spark plug, too. If he isn't sparking, the team just goes into a stall."

Tom Joyce shook his head savagely.

"That's the trouble, Jocko! Maybe I've counted too much on Hadley. Maybe I've made a big mistake in building my offense around one man." The coach's voice went moody. "I never did it before, Jocko, but Lord knows I certainly had no other choice this year. That keeper play was just made for Hadley and Slade." He fell silent, then he said, "Tell you what I'll do. I think I'll give Hadley a day off tomorrow. Maybe *he's* the one who's gone stale."

Coach Joyce could not have made a more unfortunate decision.

The one thing that Win Hadley did not need in his present unhappy state of mind was spare time. He spent that Friday afternoon wandering from place to place in Dixboro, fretting everywhere he went. He hiked out to the sawmill, and then, when he saw Mr. Slade come out into the lumber yard to speak to one of the foremen, he realized why his feet had brought him there. He wanted to rush up to him and tell him the whole story. He's such a fine man, he assured himself, he's certain to understand. But, then, Win held himself back. He realized how clever Dan Slade really was. Fine a man as he was, Owen Slade could never be expected to believe that his son could be such a rotten sport.

Sorrowfully, Win Hadley turned and trudged back to town.

He stopped in to see Walt, but his brother was busy at his desk.

"Can't shoot the breeze with you, now, Win," Walter said. "I've got all these specifications to work out for the Slade deal. You know, Mr. Slade wants quite a bit of special equipment built into these vehicles. It's going to take a bit longer than I thought, writing up the contracts."

Though Walter's manner was far from brusque,

Win could tell that his brother was anxious to see him out of his office. So he said, "Okay, Walt, sorry to have interrupted you," and left his brother to his papers.

He walked down to the Malt Shop and looked inside. The place was deserted. Everybody would be out at the athletic field. He stood alone on the sidewalk, feeling forlorn and bewildered.

Because he was a strong-minded youth, and proud, he felt that he had no one to go to. He thought, mistakenly, that he had to work out his problem singlehanded, and that neither his mother, his brother, Mr. Slade, Coach Joyce or any of his friends would be able to help him without somehow hurting themselves.

So he kept it all within himself, and by the time the whistle blew for the kickoff against Framton, Win Hadley felt that he had a stomach full of fluttering butterflies.

And he fumbled the kickoff!

The ball bounced off his chest high into the air, and as he ran to recover it, he could see the Framton players swarming down on him. Their orange-and-blue peppermint-striped sleeves and stockings flashed so as they ran that they gave the impression that there were twice as many of them as there actually were.

"For Pete's sake, grab that ball!" Teddy Scholari shouted, as he bundled himself into a ball and launched himself at a big, heavy Framton tackler.

Win stooped to grab it, but the pigskin took a crazy bounce. It slithered off his outstretched fingers and rolled back toward the goal. He whirled and dived for it, curling up with it in his arms just as a half dozen Framton players hit him from all sides.

Well, he had recovered his own fumble, but when he got to his feet and saw the ball was resting on his own 9, Win didn't feel like cheering.

On the bench, Coach Joyce closed his eyes and said to Jocko Williams, "If there's any team I hate to play, it's the one that took a shellacking the week before."

"You're right, Tom," Jocko said. "Your own boys are overconfident, and the other kids are out to redeem themselves."

The Framton Indians were doing just that. They were playing a savage game, evidently determined to wipe out the disgrace of their 45–0 loss to Crawford the week before.

On three plays, the Cougars could get no farther than their own 16. With fourth and three to go, Win went back to kick. He got off an average punt which went out of bounds on his own 45, and the Indians took over at that point.

Coach Joyce's jaw dropped when he saw the Framton boys line up in a spread something like the one in the accompanying diagram:

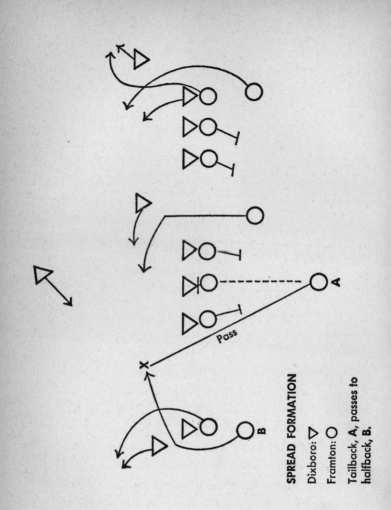

SPREAD FORMATION

Dixboro: ▷

Framton: ◯

Tailback, **A**, passes to halfback, **B**.

It was obviously intended for only one thing— to open up the Cougar defenses for a passing game, and when Coach Joyce saw it, he groaned and said, "Oh, Lord, they're loaded for bear!"

On the first play, all five eligible pass-receivers swarmed downfield. The center of the Dixboro line charged. But the passer was so far back that by the time they reached him he had coolly thrown a short, six-yarder to his right halfback cutting in.

The next play, the passer faked to the left and threw a screen pass to the quarterback who had been stationed to the right behind most of the Framton linemen. He got only four yards, because Archie had charged up from his linebacking spot to break up the play, but it was enough for a first down.

So it went, as the Indians moved steadily downfield. A five-yard pass play here, an incomplete forward there, and then a quick shoot of six or seven yards to gain the first down.

"They won't run it at all!" Coach Joyce groaned. "They know they've got no ground attack. Their only hope is to take to the air."

But, as often happens to such lopsided offenses, the Framton passing game backfired. They had moved to the Dixboro 18, completing five out of nine passes. The Cougar fans were pleading, "Hold 'em, Cougars, hold 'em!" as the center snap again went to the passer, ten to twelve yards behind the line.

Matt Hughes was off his toes the moment the ball was passed. He came barreling in, and then he stopped short. At the very moment that the passer whipped one of his flat shoots straight down the field, big Matt went high in the air. The ball struck him in the stomach. "Ooof!" went Matt, but as he came back down and hit the ground with a thud, he had both hands firmly around that ball!

First down, ten to go for the Cougars, on their own 23-yard stripe!

"C'mon, gang, let's go, let's go!" Matt pleaded in the huddle, gazing appealingly at his friend, Win Hadley. "Heck, Crawford only used their first team for one half against these guys!"

There were growls of assent from the other linemen, and Win shook himself like a man coming out of a spell.

"Okay. Dan on a cross-back left. Let's go!"

Win felt better as he grasped the football with a sure grip and slammed it into Dan Slade's belly. The Cougar halfback hit the line running low. He seemed halted temporarily, but he slithered off the hip of the Framton lineman who had stopped him, and hit daylight the moment he turned left end. He got fifteen yards and a first down.

"That's the spirit; keeper right, on five!" Win barked as they huddled again.

He took the hike from Archie and ran for a hole opening between guard and tackle. The Framton guard leaped over Bill Keller's shoulder and got one hand on Win, enough to turn him around. Win shook him off and dropped back. Both Red and Al had gone downfield, but the Indians were taking no chances on Al. They had him covered. Red, however, was free. Win hit him with a wobbly, desperation pass that he just managed to get off before the determined Framton guard rode him to the earth.

It was good for twelve yards and another first down.

The Cougar stands at last came to life.

"Our team is red-hot!" the cheerleaders yelled. "Our team is red-hot!"

The next play, Teddy Scholari followed Archie, Bill Keller and Matt Hughes for a six-yard ramble, and then Win called the keeper right again. The same situation developed as before, but this time, Win faked the pass and lateraled out to Dan, who picked up six more yards.

First down again, on the Indian 38.

"C'mon, you guys," the Framton captain shouted at his teammates. "Tighten up in there! Get that quarterback before he can get rid of the ball!"

As though to show that he practiced what he preached, on the very next play, the Framton captain dived over the line of scrimmage and nailed

Win! But he failed to pin his arms, as he had hoped to, and as Win's knees began to buckle, he wrenched his arms free and lateraled out to Dan Slade.

There was a roar from the crowd.

It couldn't have been done better if it had been planned that way, for the Framton captain's seemingly splendid defensive play had led his own teammates to let down their guard. They thought that Win had been dropped for a loss. They weren't ready for it when Dan Slade streaked into the open, lugging the ball. They tried to recover, but Dan had too much of a head start. The safety man was the only player who could get a crack at him. But as Dan sprinted down the right side lines, Al Jacobson, already downfield, got between him and the Framton safety. And Dan set him up beautifully for Al's flying block.

He made a shoulder feint as though he were going to cut to his left. The Framton man swerved. Dan cut back to the right, and Al cross-blocked the man's exposed left hip. They both went down and Dan went thundering on to a touchdown.

"Slade, Slade, rah, rah, rah!" the cheerleaders screamed, turning tailspins and throwing their black-and-gold megaphones up above their heads. Handfuls of torn paper were flying up into the air, and the band was blaring away at the Victory

March again. Up in the stands, old-time Dixboro fans were exchanging glances of pride.

"Looks like Tom Joyce may get that League title back in town, after all," one man said to another.

Down on the field, Dan Slade was actually strutting as he tossed the pigskin to the referee for placement for the point-after-touchdown try. He was almost gloating as he ran back for the huddle. Passing Win Hadley, he gave him a superior pat on the back, and hissed out of the corner of his mouth, "Nice going! I knew you'd see the light, Hadley."

Win was stunned.

For a moment, all the sounds and sights of the football field were blotted from his senses. Dan Slade thought that he had fallen in with his dirty scheme! In the huddle, all Win could see before him was Dan's arrogant face. He had to hold his hands behind his back to keep from smashing at it. He was so furious that he was still trembling when he knelt on the gridiron to take Archie's pass from center for placement for Matt, and he fumbled the ball slightly before he did.

That was all the Framton captain needed. He burst between Archie and Charley Bantam and smothered Matt's kick with his big body.

A groan rose from the Dixboro stands, but then it gave way to a fresh storm of cheers, and the man who had predicted a League championship for the Cougars nudged his neighbor and said, "Too bad, but the way our boys are going, I doubt if one point is going to be missed much."

He was a bad prophet.

As the game wore on, and the first quarter turned into the first half, and then the third period began, that one point came to be missed more and more. That was because the Cougar attack had stalled completely. Time after time, Win Hadley called the keeper play to the right, and time after time he either ran the ball himself or attempted to pass downfield. He was so blinded by his resentment of Dan Slade's smug confidence in his treachery that he could think of nothing but showing the other boy just how wrong he could be. "So I've seen the light, eh?" Win would mutter to Dan as the team broke out of every huddle, and then he would take the ball, fake a lateral and either slam off-tackle or drop back to pass. It became so monotonous that the Framton forwards were ready for Win on almost every play, piling him up at the line of scrimmage or rushing him on his pass attempts.

And while the Dixboro offensive was sputtering out, Framton's began to catch fire.

Only the crashing line-play of Matt Hughes and Charley Bantam, plus a series of damaging penalties against the Indians, kept Framton from pushing over the tying touchdown in the first half.

But when the third period began, they quickly showed the dead-silent Dixboro stands that they were not going to be denied this time.

Taking the kickoff and returning it to their own 22, the Indians swept downfield with their passer clicking on two completions out of every three attempts. He consistently hit his fast-breaking halfbacks on short shoots into the flat, and because he had grown used to Matt and Charley's charging tactics, he was able to evade them twice for good running gains up the middle.

Then, with the ball on the Dixboro 41, the passer took up his customary position ten to twelve yards behind the line. He ran back two steps and brought his arm forward as though passing to his right halfback who was covered by Dan Slade. Dan started forward, eager to intercept, and as he did so, the Framton right half turned on the steam and got behind him. The passer ran to his right to elude Matt and Charley, jumping high into the air and heaving with all his might when he saw that his man had gotten behind Dan. It was a beautiful, high spiral that must have traveled 40 or 45 yards in the air before the Framton receiver took it over his shoulder on the 9 and raced over the goal for the tying six-pointer!

Now, the importance of that fumbled pass from center and missed point loomed larger than ever as the blue-and-orange Indians lined up for their all-important attempt to take the lead.

"Block that kick! Block that kick!" the Dixboro rooters chanted, raising such a roar that the referee had to plead with them for silence to enable the Framton players to hear their own quarterback's signals.

The ball was snapped.

It was touched down and the passer quickly stepped forward and swung his foot.

The ball went high and true, the referee wheeled and threw his hands high, there was a roar of "It's good!" from the Framton stands, and the Indians went out in front, 7 to 6.

That's how the score remained as the third period ended and the fourth began. Even though Win Hadley had by then recovered from his damaging anger, it was too late. Something had happened to the Framton linemen. They fought like tigers. They rushed Win so badly that it made no difference whom he gave the ball to any more. And with that precious one-point lead to protect, the Framton coach immediately ordered his team to drop the spread and play possession football out of an old-fashioned single wing. They never passed again, and sometimes they kicked on third down. They were taking no chances on losing the ball in their own territory.

The game became that dullest of all football

contests, a kicking game. Dixboro, too, began punting on third down, hoping that Win Hadley's soaring spirals might lead to recovery of an enemy fumble.

Perhaps the biggest upset of the Western Massachusetts Scholastic League season was in the making, when, with less than three minutes to go, Gabby Windham was spilled for a one-yard loss on a screen-pass play to the left, and Win Hadley had to go back to his own 33-yard line for a fourth-down punt. There were seven yards to go, and it would have been sheer recklessness to try for a first down so deep in their own territory and with that much time remaining. The only thing to do was to punt, and play for a break.

With the wind at his back, Win got off his best punt of the season. It rose on a sharp spiral, and as it arched over, it fell with terrific speed. The Framton safety, seeing the wind start to play tricks with the ball, wisely decided not to risk catching it. He let it fall. It bounced all the way down to his own 20.

A good break, but still, it was Framton's ball.

Slowly, trying to "eat up the clock," the Indians ran off two line plays. There was now less than two minutes to go. As they huddled, Matt Hughes ran over to Archie and little Charley.

"They'll kick on third down," he panted. "We've got to block it! Here, Archie, you and I will submarine the center and guard. You go over us, Charley, and get the kicker."

The big center and the game little guard both nodded, and, sure enough, as the Framton boys came slowly out of their huddle, they were lining up in punt formation. The ball was passed, both Archie and Matt dived at the feet of the men before them, spilling them—and Charley Bantam dashed into the enemy backfield. He came in low, but as the blockers went for him, he hurled himself into the air and sailed over their heads.

Thud-bam!

The two sounds in quick succession were of the punter's foot meeting the ball and the ball meeting the front of Charley Bantam's helmet.

"Blocked kick!" the fans screamed, as the ball rose into the air and settled into the happy arms of Red McGinley, who had come charging in from left end.

Though Charley Bantam had been knocked groggy, he still managed to grin with delight as he was helped from the field. That was because it was Dixboro's ball, first and ten on the Framton 24— and there was a minute and five seconds left to play!

There was pandemonium on both sides of the field as the rejuvenated Cougars raced to the line of scrimmage. The moment they got there, Archie bent quickly and passed the ball to Win without waiting for a signal. It took Framton by surprise. In an instant, Win had darted past the Framton center into enemy territory. He sprinted to the 13 before he was brought down.

First down, forty-five seconds to go!

Now, the desperate Cougars didn't even huddle. Win shouted his instructions as he ran back into position.

"Gabby on a dive—ball!" he shouted, and the line surged.

No gain. Twenty-seven seconds to go!

"Ball!" Win shouted as they scrambled into position, and he took the pigskin, jumped and hit Al Jacobson crossing over on the 7. Seventeen seconds left!

"Matt, on a field goal!" he yelled, running back to the 17 and kneeling down. He could count the seconds ticking off as his weary teammates struggled to get into position. Ten seconds to go—nine, eight, seven, six . . .

"Ball!" he screamed.

Back it came, down it went—up loomed big Matt, and there was the impact of his foot meeting the ball and the pigskin was spinning out from under Win Hadley's right index finger. It flew end-over-end right between the uprights, and as a tremendous shout rose from the Dixboro stands, Win had both arms around his big friend and was hugging him for dear life.

Not half a minute later, the Dixboro Victory March was blaring over the field as the gun ended the game with the score Dixboro 9, Framton 7. A delirious bunch of Dixboro Cougars hoisted Matt Hughes on their shoulders and carried him off to the locker room.

But their shouts of jubilation died in their throats the moment they clattered inside and saw the furious, bleak face of Coach Tom Joyce.

"What makes you think you've got something to shout about?" the angry coach blazed at them. "There!" he continued, shaking with rage and pointing a finger out the door toward the disappointed Framton Indians who were walking dejectedly toward the fieldhouse. "There are the boys who have something to shout about! They outplayed you all the way! And you were lucky to win! And if you keep on playing the way you played today, you'll be lucky if you win another game." He drew breath and wheeled on a shamefaced Win Hadley. "You! You'll be quarterbacking the second team, starting Monday!"

Without another word, Coach Tom Joyce strode from a now-silent room.

The next thing Win Hadley heard was the voice of Dan Slade snarling into his ear, "And as far as I'm concerned, Mr. Second-string ball-hog, the bad news has only just started."

CHAPTER ELEVEN

Win Shows His Stuff

WIN HADLEY and Matt Hughes walked home from Dixboro High's athletic field in silence.

It wasn't until they had turned into Elm Street that the brooding quiet was broken by a loud sigh from big Matt.

"You know, Win," he said, "I've always dreamed of this day, the day when I'd be the hero. But, somehow," he went on, ruefully shaking his head, "somehow it doesn't feel good at all."

Win looked at his faithful friend sadly.

"I know, Matt—and I, I'm sorry it had to be spoiled by me."

"Oh, come on!" Matt cried, shoving his friend playfully, trying to recapture their old lighthearted relationship. "Things aren't that bad, you know. You won't be on that second team more than one day. Coach just lost his temper, that's all."

Win shook his head.

"Uh-uh—you know better than that, Matt. I never saw Coach Joyce so mad! And he was right, too. I played like a swell-head all afternoon, and I darn near lost the game for us."

Matt Hughes paused and studied his friend. His honest face was sober.

"To tell the truth, Win, you did. But, why? Gee, you're no swell-head! What got into you?"

Win Hadley looked away. He felt like crying. But he just couldn't tell his friend how stupid he had been in letting Dan Slade get under his skin. Besides, the whole business was so confused now, and sordid, that he didn't want to talk about it. When he turned to face Matt again, his eyes were blank and friendless.

"Well," he said wearily, as they came in front of his house, "here's where I get off."

He went up the walk slowly, and Matt Hughes noticed that for the first time in many months, his friend did not hurdle the hedge and wheel to ask the familiar question, "See you tonight?" And big Matt's heart was almost as heavy as Win's as he walked on to his own home.

Win Hadley's downcast mood lasted throughout dinner, and it was almost matched by the grave demeanor of his brother and his mother. No one spoke, although Walter and Mrs. Hadley occasion-

ally exchanged glances of concern at Win's unhappy face. At last, after Win had laid down his
knife and fork with half of his dinner uneaten and
had been excused from the table, Walter rose to
follow him into the living room.

"What's wrong, Win?" he asked gently, as his
young brother dropped listlessly into an armchair.

Win's reply was to stare into space.

"Come on, Win," his brother went on, his voice
sharpening. "Something must be wrong, boy. I
never saw you play such a terrible game before.
Why, for a while out there, it looked as if you were
deliberately hogging the ball."

Win Hadley jumped to his feet, his face whiten-
ing. He clenched his hands into two tight fists and
he stammered, "Don't, Walt. Please, don't. . . .
Honestly, if another person says that to me, I'm
going to hit him. I don't care who it is! Even . . .
even you, Walt . . ."

Walter Hadley peered into his brother's tense,
white face. Slowly, fondly, he pushed him back
into his chair. He drew up another chair to sit
alongside.

"Take it easy, Win," he said. Then, laying an
affectionate hand on Win's knee, he continued,
"The worst thing a man can do with his troubles,
Win, is to keep them to himself. That's something
most men don't learn until they go out in the

world. But you can save yourself a lot of grief if you learn it now." He leaned back. "Now, let's have it."

Win looked up in anguish. Finally, after a long quivering sigh, he gulped down a big mouthful of air and in a low voice, he began to speak.

"All right, Walt—here it is."

Then he told his brother all about Dan Slade's threats to ruin the important deal with Mr. Slade. As Walter Hadley listened, it was his face that began to turn white with anger. The moment Win finished, Walter Hadley leaped erect and hurried into the hall to seize the telephone. He began dialing. Win hastened after him.

"Whom are you calling, Walt?"

"Owen Slade," Walter replied, his lips tight and grim.

"But, but, Walt—I thought of that, too. Would it do any good?"

Walter Hadley frowned. Reluctantly, he restored the telephone to its cradle. He shook his head.

"No, I guess it wouldn't. Almost any father in the world would demand proof of such a story as this one, I guess, and Owen Slade is no exception." He struck his hands together fiercely. "Proof! If only we had proof! Imagine his trying to do such a thing to you!"

"But, Walt, why worry so much about me? What

about the deal? Aren't you worried that Dan will wreck that?"

Walter Hadley shrugged.

"Not too much, Win. The worst that boy can do is tip off some of the other agencies. Of course, they'll contact Mr. Slade with offers right away. But the fact is, I'll have a two-week jump on them. They won't be getting all those specifications drawn up in a hurry, and if Mr. Slade still insists on November delivery, they'll never make it."

Walter Hadley grinned encouragingly at his brother before he spoke again.

"Stop worrying, Win. The deal is important, sure. But we'll be all right. This certainly isn't a problem you have to handle. Just get out there next week and show Tom Joyce what you can really do! Remember, the Crawford game is coming along soon, and it won't do to have you fretting when that one rolls around. And for Pete's sake, don't break the family tradition. I started every game I ever played, and you'd better do the same!"

The Hadley family tradition was preserved intact by the time the next Saturday came around, and the Cougars traveled to nearby Wharton to take on the Engineers of Wharton Tech.

For when the whistle blew for the kickoff, it was Win Hadley who was holding the ball for Matt Hughes.

Throughout the week, Win had worked with a
dogged determination to prove to Coach Joyce that
he wasn't the grandstander he had seemed to be.
Stung by the double disgrace of his demotion as
quarterback and team captain, Win had turned on
the juice from the moment he had jogged onto the
practice field that Monday. He tackled viciously,
he ran with savage speed and a baffling change of
pace, he passed with such zest his receivers com-
plained of stinging hands and he called his plays
with crisp sureness. And he met the problem of
how to handle Dan Slade by treating him with a
cool courtesy that was not noticed by his teammates, but was not lost on Dan. In two days, he had
Coach Joyce thinking kindly of him again. By
Wednesday, he was back on the Varsity, running
Coach Joyce's cherished keeper.

And on the Friday night before the game, Win
Hadley got the lift of his young life when Walter
came and told him he had submitted his bid to Mr.
Slade that day. "They'll never have time to out-
maneuver me, now," he told Win gleefully, "so
your worries are over!"

As Scoop Slocum described it next day in the
Crawford Record, "Win Hadley rose to new heights
of brilliance" against Wharton Tech. From the
moment the game got under way, Win had seen
that the big Wharton line was going to be tough

to crack. It was this same line that had forced Crawford to take to the air in their 13–0 victory the week before, and once they had been forced to kick to the Cougars, they showed that they were out to play the same kind of game by shifting into a seven-man line.

Win felt them out the first three plays. He tried Teddy Scholari on his favorite pop up the middle. He gave Dan a keeper lateral to the right, and ducked over guard once himself. Net gain: eight yards.

But Win wasn't disappointed as he dropped back to punt from his own 38. He had seen that the center of Wharton Tech's 1-2-1, or diamond defense, was wide open for passes to either Red McGinley or Al Jacobson crossing over from the ends. He even smiled as he called the hike signal to Archie and let his foot ride into the ball.

The Engineers ground out a pair of first downs, chiefly on power end runs off a split T. The quarterback would lateral out to the left halfback, who would go wide and deep behind the other two backs as blockers, plus the running guard who had pulled out to lead the play. At first, they just rode Red McGinley and Gabby Windham into the ground. But after Matt Hughes shifted over into leftside linebacker, the Wharton Tech running game ground to a halt. Matt charged the interference that Red desperately fought wide, giving Teddy Scholari plenty of time to come up and make the tackles.

Just before the quarter ended, the Engineers punted and Win put his strategy into practice.

On the very first play, he shot a perfect pass to Al Jacobson who had gone straight downfield and then looped back up the middle. He hit Al again on a jump, switched to Red McGinley on a long pass to the left—and then fooled the Engineers completely by handing off to Gabby Windham on a draw play.

High-stepping Gabby galloped down to the Wharton Tech 45 before he was stopped.

In the huddle, Win clapped his hands together gleefully and said to Al Jacobson, "Get on your high horse, Al—I'm going to try a long one down the middle."

Al nodded and lined up split wide to the right. Win took the snap, faked another draw to Teddy and faded far back. He needed time for Al to get out there, so he scooted to his left as though he had decided to run the ball. It drew the Engineer defenses over. Then, with Teddy and Archie and Matt blocking for him manfully, Win ran back to his right and threw it straight down the middle.

It was Al Jacobson's best play. He had been going downfield, side by side with the Wharton safety. But he was holding something back. The moment he saw Win let fly, he turned it on. He beat the safety by a full step, plucked the ball out of the air, arched his back to shake off a desperation shoestring tackle and breezed on for the touchdown.

Though the Cougars only scored once more as they went on to a 14–3 victory, the final tally did not fully reflect the splendid passing show staged by Win Hadley. He completed fifteen passes out of twenty-nine attempts, and he and Al Jacobson would have had another touchdown to their credit had not Matt Hughes been off side on a third scoring pass.

As could be expected, big Matt was almost weeping as the two jubilant friends walked home from Station Square, where the team bus had discharged the triumphant Cougars to the repeated cheers of their followers.

"Gee, I sure did botch that one up for you," Matt moaned. "Me and my two left feet."

"Who cares?" Win said, laughing. "We won, didn't we? And besides, how about what you kept me from botching up last week?"

Matt grinned.

"Yeah, but that was last week. The fans don't remember that far back, Win."

"Good thing they don't. And maybe we had better forget about today, too. We've got Crawford coming up next week."

The faces of the two friends became serious.

"I sure wish we were playing them on Thanksgiving, the way we always did," Win went on. "Those League schedule changes are working in their favor."

"How do you mean?"

"Well, I don't think we've really got the kinks worked out of that keeper play yet. I mean, if we played the rest of the W.M.S.L. teams before we played Crawford, we'd be ready for them."

"Heck, Win—you've got the keeper worked out pretty good, I'd say."

Win Hadley frowned.

"We haven't tried all the possibilities yet. For instance, Dan Slade's never tried to pass to Al from it."

Matt shook his head and grinned wryly.

"What? Get Dan Slade to throw the ball to somebody else? You're dreaming!"

Win smiled and said, "Oh, I don't know. Didn't you see how quiet Dan was after today's game? I've got an idea he's changed."

"Why?" Matt asked, a puzzled expression on his face.

"Oh, I don't know," Win said mysteriously. "Maybe he's decided that he has a conscience, after all."

"You know something!" Matt said, turning eagerly on his friend. "Come on, spill it."

"Well," Win started to say, deciding that the time had finally come to tell his friend about what had been going on, but then he heard a cheerful voice behind them say, "Yeah, Win, that's the idea —spill it!"

To Win's horror, the speaker was Scoop Slocum. He had bounced up behind them unheard, and now, from the expression of mirth on Scoop's bright face, Win could guess that he had heard every word they had been saying since they had turned down Elm Street. For a moment, Win stood in crimson confusion, until Matt saved the day with a good-natured explosion.

"Tell you?" Matt shouted. "It'd be safer telling it to a tape recorder!"

Little George grinned and said, "Aw, come on, fellows—how do you expect me to get to college if you hold out on me like that?"

"How do you mean, Scoop?" Win asked.

"Well, the *Crawford Record* pays me two dollars for every story of mine they accept. So if you've got a good yarn on Dan Slade, that means with today's game story I'd be making four dollars."

Win and Matt couldn't believe their ears.

"Put yourself through college on four dollars a week?" they both shouted. "Are you crazy?"

Scoop Slocum grinned again and winked.

"Well, you see, fellows," he chirped, "it's not a very big college." Then he stepped back a pace with an expression of mock ferocity on his face, and growled, "Out of my way, you big bohunks, or else I'll be too late to tell the world about what we're going to do to Crawford next week." Jamming a pencil in his hatband, snapping up the brim of his hat, he darted between them and ran down the sidewalk, bawling: "Stop the press! Stop the press!"

Matt grinned at Win, and said, "He's a nut, all right, but I love him!"

"Me, too," Win said, laughing, as he leaped the front hedge of his home. "See you tonight?"

Matt nodded and began trotting down Elm Street to his own house.

CHAPTER TWELVE

Thief in the Night

WIN HADLEY was in high spirits as he ate dinner that night.

He had not felt so elated, so confident, since football practice began.

Everything seemed to be going right.

First, Walter's deal appeared to be safe. Second, all the fellows on the Varsity seemed to have gotten over their minor peeve about publicity and were playing together as one team. Finally, even Dan Slade seemed to have forgotten about his threat to "get even."

Probably, Win thought, absently lifting a forkful of juicy steak to his mouth, probably Dan's auto agency friends found out about Walt's head start on the fleet order and decided not to try to horn in.

Certainly Dan had been awfully subdued after today's game. He didn't act like a fellow with a grudge, and Win had found few enough chances to feed Dan the ball against those big Engineers. That last thought made Win wince a bit and lay a hand on his bruised left ribs. Those big linemen had sure buried him on a couple of pass attempts, and there were a few of them who didn't mind piling on, either. Still, he thought, smiling, we did almost as well as Crawford did against them.

"Hey," his brother Walt said, cutting into his daydreams. "What are you mumbling to yourself and grinning about? Got money in the bank?"

"Better than that," Win said. "I was just thinking that we ought to have a pretty good chance against Crawford next week."

"If you pass like you did today, you'll beat them," Walt said. "I hear you can run more against Crawford than Wharton Tech—and with a passing game to help you open them up, you should really move!" Walter looked over at their mother, sitting proudly between them. "And by next Saturday night we should have a double reason to celebrate," he added. "By that time, I should have the Slade contract signed, sealed and delivered. If Hattie weren't such a good scout, I don't think I'd have made it. She's taking the week off to go to her niece's wedding in Michigan, but she worked last night and came in early this morning before train time to finish it up for me. What a gal!"

"Boy!" Win exclaimed, reaching for a second

baked potato. "Things are sure looking up, aren't they?"

If Win Hadley could have been within sight of the Owen Slade Sawmill Company property about three or four hours later that night, he might not have been so happy. For if he had been there, and kept his eyes peeled, he would have seen a white sport car coast down the hill with silent motor and slide to a cautious halt in the shadows cast by the trees.

In an instant, a tall, well-built figure, wearing a peaked cap pulled low, leaped softly from the car and began to move on tiptoe toward the plant gate. As he moved, the intruder reached into his pocket for a key. In another instant, there was a light scratching of metal on metal as he inserted the key in the lock. Then, the gate swung open on squeaking hinges and the figure darted inside, swiftly and carefully closing the gate behind him.

For a moment, the figure kept to the dark pools of shadow cast by the fence and gate to his rear. Then, gathering himself, pulling the cap still lower, he was racing up the driveway with amazing speed, heading for the smallest of the Slade buildings which housed the business offices.

He ran so swiftly and so surely up that brick-bordered road that a wise observer would have had no trouble deducing two facts. These were that the intruder was an athlete and that he knew his surroundings. If Win Hadley had been the observer, he would have guessed in an instant that it was Dan Slade!

It was Dan, all right, and he lost no time in inserting a second key into the front door of the office building. He slipped inside and disappeared.

Within the building, Dan pulled a flashlight from his pocket. He snapped it on. A beam of light leaped down the corridor before him. In alarm, Dan shielded it with his left hand and began creeping down the hall to his father's office at the end.

Once he had reached it, he selected a third key from the key case he held. He smiled as he did, for he had a fourth—the key to his father's desk!

This he used the moment he had gained access to the office. Congratulating himself on having filched the keys from his father's jacket while Mr. Slade was taking a shower that evening, Dan pulled the middle desk drawer open and stealthily began holding up its contents to the light of his flashlight. Coming upon a thick, folded paper, he gasped with delight when he saw the printing on the outside of it. It read:

AGREEMENT

between

The Owen Slade Sawmill Company

and

The Dixboro Automobile Agency

Panting with excitement, Dan quickly flipped through the pages. He saw detail after detail concerning the forthcoming contract between his father and Walter Hadley's company, and then, turning it over, he saw Walter Hadley's signature on the back, below a blank line where his father was supposed to sign, making the contract effective. Smiling, he slipped it into his inside coat pocket. This was just what he had come for!

Noticing a bulky duplicate of the contract in the drawer, he stooped and took that, too! He made sure there was nothing else and then he restored the other papers to his father's desk, closed the drawers, locked them and pulled a handkerchief from his pocket to wipe all fingerprints from the desk. This done, he snapped off his light, let himself out—and within another minute he was back in his sport car, almost shouting aloud with wicked laughter as he released the brake and quietly rolled away from the scene of his crime.

Monday morning, Walter Hadley was thunderstruck to receive a telephone call from Owen Slade, and to hear him say, "Say, Hadley, did you give me those contracts of yours yet?"

"Certainly, Mr. Slade! I left them for you on Saturday morning myself. Didn't you get them?"

"Now that you mention it, I believe I did. But, confound it, Hadley! I can't seem to locate them."

Walter Hadley's insides turned over.

"You—you can't find them, sir?"

"Devil take it, I thought I shoved them in my desk drawer before I took off. But they're not there! Oh, well, they'll turn up somewhere, I guess. No cause to worry, Hadley. You've got your carbon copy, I'm sure. If we can't find them, why you can just make up another set. Eh?"

Walter gulped. With Hattie away, that little chore would be no joke. Still, if he had to . . . "Why, that would be perfectly all right, Mr. Slade. You're sure you don't have your copies, though?"

"No, I'm not really sure. They may turn up yet. I'll check around some more and call you back in a day or so. Right?"

"Right, Mr. Slade. Goodbye." Walter hung up, a worried frown on his face.

Fifteen minutes later, after some increasingly frantic searching, Walter knew that a bad situation had become immeasurably worse. He did not have the third copy—the one that should have been in the office files. He forced himself to sit still and try to reconstruct all that had happened on Saturday morning. . . . Hattie had been in a mad rush to finish the typing of the complicated specifications . . . he had offered to drive her to Crawford, where she could get the through train . . . he had dashed in to the Slade Sawmill office on the way and dropped the contracts off with Mr. Slade's secretary . . . that was it! He leaned back and groaned as realization came to him.

He and Hattie had both been in such a tearing hurry that all three copies—the two that he had signed and that Mr. Slade should sign, as well as the third that should have stayed in the files—had been bundled together and slipped into the big envelope. And now Mr. Slade might have lost them all. What a mess!

He could just imagine trying to explain to Mr. Slade that he didn't have a copy to refer to. What kind of businessman would Mr. Slade think him? A fine impression *that* would make!

But how the devil could they be lost? He'd given them to Mr. Slade's secretary and she had distinctly said she would hand them to Mr. Slade at once, knowing how important they were. As Walt sat there, recalling Owen Slade's saying he vaguely remembered shoving them into the drawer, he also remembered something else—Dan Slade's threat to Win. Could that—could *that* possibly be the explanation? It just might be.

With difficulty he restrained himself from rushing right over to the school. He waited until lunchtime when he knew he would find the boys in the school cafeteria.

Dan Slade saw Walter first.

"There's your big brother, Hadley," he called

to Win. "Seems to be looking for something." Win whirled and saw Walter in the doorway, surveying the large room. He glanced back at Dan and saw him wink and heard him say, "Sure hope it hasn't got anything to do with that big deal of his."

Shooting Dan Slade a furious glance, Win left his table and hurried to greet his brother.

"Walt!" he cried, seeing his white face and tightened lips. "What's happened?"

"Plenty," Walt said grimly. "Mr. Slade has lost the contracts."

Win's mouth flew open in alarm. He turned, involuntarily, and saw that Dan Slade was watching them, a cocky smirk on his face.

"Yes, Win," Walter said, evenly, his glance following his brother's. "That's why I came down here. Do you think Dan had anything to do with it?"

Win turned back to Walter. His pulse was beating fast, but he could still think.

"Yes, I think he could have, Walt." Win's voice was low and vibrant with concern. "Just before I came over to you, he made some crack about your looking for something. I didn't pay any attention. But then he said he hoped it didn't have anything to do with your deal." Win's voice broke. He clenched his fists and felt his eyes go moist with tears of helpless rage. He gritted his teeth, and said,

"Oh, how I'd love to go back there and beat the truth out of him!"

"Careful, now, boy," Walt said, laying a hand on Win's arm. "That won't do any good. The only thing for you to do is to pretend that nothing's happened." Seeing his brother stiffen and stick out his jaw, Walter continued, "I know it's going to be tough to do, but you've got to do it! Play dumb, Win! Butter him up! Pretend nothing's happened. And in the meantime, I'll see what I can do about preparing another set of contracts for Mr. Slade."

Win turned, his eyes full of hope.

"Oh, Walt! Can you?"

"Well," Walter said grimly, squaring his jaw, "I'm sure going to try."

Then he wheeled and walked rapidly back to his car.

But when Walter Hadley drove out to see a prospect that afternoon, he passed the Owen Slade Sawmill Company, and even his fighting spirit hit absolute rock bottom when he saw the business car drawn up outside. On the door of the automobile was the name of the company. It was:

SQUARE DEAL MOTORS, INC.

Walter drove the rest of the way in the deepest gloom. He would not tell Win, but he had seen enough to know that the vultures were gathering already.

Even though Walter Hadley kept his vow not to let Win gain any hint of how bad things really were becoming, Win had learned enough to begin to worry again. And he had seen enough of Walter's solemn face throughout Monday night to be twice as concerned by the time Tuesday practice rolled around.

During dummy scrimmage, he started running a keeper play to the right and suddenly stopped dead with a vacant expression on his face.

Coach Joyce's whistle blew.

"What's the matter with you, son?" the coach asked. "Get your signals mixed?"

"No, Coach. I—I just seemed to forget what I was going to do."

Coach Joyce shot Win a puzzled look before blowing his whistle again and shouting, "All right —let's try it again."

This time, Win executed the play correctly. He faked a run and lateraled off to Dan Slade.

"Good," Coach Joyce yelled from the side lines, cupping his hands to his mouth. "Now, let's try that triple reverse."

This was a special play that Coach Joyce had dreamed up for the Crawford game, and it was as difficult as it was tricky. Actually, it was a double reverse with a lateral on the end of it. Win would pretend that he still had the ball and drop back as though to pass. As he did this, Dan would give it to Gabby Windham, coming around to the right. Then, Win would delay two counts and start left himself, and Gabby would turn and lateral to him. The play had two purposes: first, to confuse the opponents, and, second, to make them think that they had figured it out as a double reverse to the right. Then, a man apparently out of the play would appear from nowhere going to the left.

So the Varsity lined up, prepared to rehearse this play once more. Win Hadley took the ball, spun, handed to Dan as he was supposed to, and then, to the utter amazement of everyone on the field, he stood as though dazed while poor Gabby took the ball from Dan and looked wildly about for someone to lateral to.

Again the whistle blew.

"Okulski," Coach Joyce shouted, "go in there for Hadley." Then he turned and yelled to Win, "Come over here, boy. I want to talk to you."

Red-faced, Win trotted over and sat down beside the kindly Dixboro coach.

"Something's bothering you, boy," Coach Joyce said gently. "It has been all season. What is it?"

Win looked away, and the coach went on, "Anything to do with me, son?"

Win shook his head. Then he turned and faced Coach Joyce.

"It's, it's a family matter, Coach. Honest. I promise you, I'll get over it in a day or two."

"You'd better, boy," Coach Joyce said, shaking his head sadly. "If you don't, we won't have much chance to beat Crawford."

The next day was Wednesday and Walter Hadley could no longer stand the suspense. He telephoned Owen Slade.

"Glad you called, Hadley," Mr. Slade boomed. "Just about to call you myself."

"Yes, sir?"

"Well, the confounded truth is that I can't find those contracts of yours. Searched high and low for them, high and low. Sorry, and all that, but if you'll just shoot a fresh set over to me I'll get this thing over with." Walter's heart sank as Owen Slade boomed on. "It'll be to your advantage to get them to me as soon as possible, Hadley. Fact is, another auto outfit's been over to see me. Interested in the same deal. But I'm holding them off, Hadley, because I like the way you do business."

There was more, but Walter Hadley barely heard it. At last, in a weak voice, he interrupted to ask, "Sir, are you sure you really lost the contracts?"

"Eh, Hadley—what's that?"

Walter had noted the tone of annoyance in Mr. Slade's voice, but he went on.

"I mean, do you think they might have been stolen?"

Owen Slade's voice rose in astonishment.

"Stolen? Hadley, get a grip on yourself! Just do as I say, and— Why, what would anyone want with a set of worthless contracts? Who would steal them?"

It was on the tip of Walter Hadley's tongue to retort, "Your own son!" But he held back just in time. That would only ruin everything. Instead, he tried to make his voice brisk as he said, "I'll get those contracts to you, sir."

"That's the ticket, Hadley. Remember—Friday at the latest!"

Walter hung up, and then he placed his head in his hands. Friday at the latest! Not even two full days—and Hattie away. He'd never be able to meet Owen Slade's deadline.

Next day, Thursday, Win Hadley came listlessly into the fieldhouse and found the way to his locker blocked by a smirking Dan Slade.

"You got something you want to tell me, Hadley?" Dan asked, winking.

"Such as what?" Win countered.

"Don't be cute. You get me, well enough. I repeat: You got something to tell me?"

Win looked at him coolly and said, "Yes."

Dan grinned triumphantly.

"Attaboy, Hadley, now you're on the beam. What is it?"

Win Hadley pointed down at Dan Slade's feet

and, in a cold voice, said, "I just want to tell you that your shoelace is untied." Then he shoved past him to his own locker and sat down. Even though he knew that Dan was furious, it didn't make him feel any better. For now he was positive that it was Dan Slade's sly hand that had removed those contracts.

Thoroughly upset, Win dressed and went out to practice. He promptly showed his state of mind by balling things up worse than he had on Tuesday, and at last a long-suffering Coach Joyce waved him over to the Scrubs and sent Emil Okulski into his place on the Varsity.

After Friday-night dinner, Win overheard his brother speaking on the telephone to Mr. Hibbert, the owner of the Dixboro Automobile Agency.

"No, sir," Walter said. "Mr. Slade was called out of town this afternoon. But he left word he would be back tomorrow morning and was expecting to hear from me."

There was a long painful pause before Walter continued: "No, sir, it really doesn't make much difference, anyway. You see, it'll be at least a week before I can write up a new set of contracts. I—I guess I've lost the deal. . . ."

Win Hadley's eyes were hot and stinging as he stumbled out into the night.

CHAPTER THIRTEEN

A Nose for News

AT THAT VERY MOMENT, however, unknown to Win, his fortunes were taking a decided turn for the better. For, at that moment, little George Slocum was walking along Main Street, Crawford, bound for the bus that would take him back to Dixboro.

He had just left the City Room of the *Crawford Record,* his favorite spot in all the world. He had left now only because the editor had told him bluntly to get out from under foot, and he had meekly obeyed, not daring to offend the great man.

Suddenly, a white sport car drew up at the curb alongside him and a voice called: "Hey, Stoop—I mean, Scoop—you want a lift back to town?"

Stung, George was about to tell Dan Slade to go peddle his papers, when he remembered that he would like to get back to Dixboro before the Malt

Shop closed. So he said, "Sure, I can use a lift. But, if you're going to keep calling me Stoop, I'd rather take a bus."

"Aw, forget it," Dan said. "I was only kidding. C'mon, hop in."

Little George clambered in alongside Dan, and the sport car roared away. As they moved through the downtown Crawford traffic, Dan glanced sideways at George and said, "You all fixed to give me a good write-up in tomorrow's game?"

Scoop frowned. "Depends on how you play."

"How come you don't feel that way about your buddy?"

"Who do you mean?"

"Aw, cut it out—you know who I mean. Win Hadley, that's who. You'd think you were his hired hand, the goo you write about him!"

Scoop Slocum flushed. He was about to tell Dan to stop and let him out. But then, some quality within him, something that newspapermen call "a nose for news," kept him in his seat, insulted though he was.

"Oh?" he said, with seeming innocence. "Supposing I write some of that—er—goo about you?"

"You'd be doing yourself a favor," Dan snapped, slamming on the brakes as a traffic light turned suddenly against him. Then his manner softened and he winked slyly. "You like sport cars, good times? Well, you just—"

"And supposing I don't?" Scoop shot out quickly, taking Dan off his guard.

"Then you'll get just what Hadley got!" Dan snarled, unable to stop himself.

Wisely, Scoop said nothing more. But, if he seemed to sit in stupid silence while a red-faced Dan Slade drove his car through crawling traffic, actually his lightning-fast brain was putting two and two together and getting the right answer. Little Scoop was recalling what Win Hadley had been saying last Saturday when he had followed him and Matt Hughes up Elm Street. He had said something about Dan Slade being "changed" and then something about his having "decided that he has a conscience, after all." Then, Scoop recalled how Win had taken a tailspin in practice that week, and how smug Dan had seemed. Now, hearing Dan threaten him with "what Hadley got," he knew in his bones that he was on the trail of something underhanded. So he let Dan get more and more uneasy about having let that remark slip out, before he began to play on his vanity.

"That's a hot one!" he said aloud, and to no one in particular. "Imagine anyone's being able to hurt Win Hadley!" He turned, looked Dan square in the eye and chuckled. "What a sense of humor!" he said.

Dan Slade's face turned as red as the stoplight they were waiting for.

"Shut up, you wise little snoop!" he snarled. "Cut the cackling or I'll bust your nose for you."

Scoop feigned shock and alarm.

"But, Dan, I thought, I mean, I—I didn't know you were serious. I thought you were just joking. I mean, after all, Win Hadley is so successful and so popular—it never—"

Dan Slade almost ran under a truck, he brought his foot down so hard on the gas pedal. He brought the car to a screeching halt, and as he did, he bellowed out of the side of his mouth: *"Shut up!"*

Chortling with inner glee, Scoop once again showed signs of fright. He shoved farther away from Dan in the seat and glanced at him fearfully. Seeing him act that way made Dan feel better, and as he drove on again, he started to hold forth.

"So that's what you think, eh? You think Hadley's too big to be hurt by the likes of me? Well, let me tell you . . ." He paused and glanced at George, and Scoop made his face go blank. "Now, don't get the idea I ever did this," Dan began slyly, "but let's just say I did want to give it to Hadley —here's what I could do."

Then, eagerly, giving himself completely away, much to the mounting disgust of Scoop Slocum, Dan Slade poured out the whole sordid scheme. Twice, during his recital of it, little George had to turn his head away to keep Dan from reading the contempt so plain on his face. At last, Dan came to the end. Momentarily, he turned to flash a look of triumph at George, but in the next instant, his expression had turned to one of deep alarm—for a black police car had suddenly pulled alongside his car. Above the sharp wail of a siren, they could hear the stern voice of a policeman calling, "Pull over to the curb, there!"

Dan stopped. He watched the policeman draw ahead of them, park, alight from his auto and walk grimly toward them. With his guilty conscience, Dan Slade began to think dire thoughts of what the officer might want. That was why, when the policeman said, "Let me see your driver's license," Dan let out a loud sigh of relief and said, "Oh, that."

The policeman raised his eyebrows.

"Oh, that, eh? Just a little matter of darting in and out of traffic like there weren't any laws at all." He stepped back and examined the flashy sport car. "Maybe you'd better show me your owner's license first."

His voice was so stern and it was so plain that he suspected that the sport car had been stolen that Dan Slade became really flustered. His breath came hard as he fumbled in his pockets for his licenses, and he stammered, "I—I can't seem to find them."

"You can't, eh?" the policeman growled. "Then you'd better follow me to headquarters."

He turned and made for his car, and as he did, the frantic Dan sent his hand diving into his inside coat pocket. It came out grasping a sheaf of papers, among them a long, official-looking document. He shuffled through them wildly.

"I've got them!" he suddenly shouted. "Here, officer, I've found them!"

But the policeman was already opening the door of his auto. Quickly, Dan hopped out, waving the licenses in his left hand. With his right, he began stuffing the other papers back into his pocket. But some of them slipped through his fumbling fingers and fell to the floor of the car. Dan didn't stop to retrieve them, however, because he was eager to reach the policeman before he drove off.

He sprinted to the police car. George Slocum saw that he had made it in time, and he was glad. He was still hopeful of getting back to Dixboro before the Malt Shop closed. For a moment, George watched as the policeman examined Dan's licenses. Then, he let his glance stray over to the spilled papers.

George Slocum caught his breath.

There, looming up in all that litter, was a large, white, folded oblong of papers. Printed across the top of it was that single damning sentence:

AGREEMENT
between
The Owen Slade Sawmill Company
and
The Dixboro Automobile Agency

What further proof did he need?

Little George's heart was beating wildly as he slid his hand toward it. He glanced at Dan. He was returning to the car! Too late, Scoop thought—I'll never get away with it. He groaned in inward dismay, but then, instantly, he had another plan. Still keeping his hand hidden, he quickly turned the contract over so that the blank side was uppermost. He wanted Dan to think it had landed that way. Then he looked out the windshield, pretending to be lost in thought. He heard Dan open the door, growling angrily, "Wise cop! Had to give me a ticket for—"

There was a sharp intake of breath from Dan Slade.

George turned to see him glaring at him, white-faced, his eyes sharp with suspicion as he pointed at the papers on the floor.

"You been snooping again?" he snarled. "You touch any of this stuff?"

"Me? What stuff?"

Scoop's face was all innocence and his eyes blank with bewilderment, as his gaze followed Dan's pointing finger.

"Oh, that—matter of fact, I never noticed it. I've been sitting here thinking of that story of yours—of how you could fix a guy like Win Hadley if you wanted to. That sure would be a smart way to do it, Dan."

Dan Slade smirked as he put the papers back in his pocket.

"Of course, I'd never do such a thing," he purred, starting the motor and pulling away from the curb. "But I just wanted to show you who was smarter than who."

Scoop nodded gravely. Then he clapped his hands against his forehead and groaned aloud.

"My record book! I forgot my record book!"

Dan stopped the car at the last light before they swung right for the Dixboro road. "What's wrong, Scoop? Hey! Where are you going?"

"Back to the *Record* office," Scoop said, grimacing as he stepped out of the car. "I left my record of all this season's games there. If I don't get back there in time, the janitor will throw it out."

"Pretty stupid if you ask me," Dan grumbled. Then, shooting a look full of angry suspicion at Scoop, he snapped, "You forget about that story I made up back there, you hear me?"

"Oh, sure, Dan. And, listen, I'm not kidding when I say I'm going to put your name in headlines."

Both boys smiled as they parted, but for vastly different reasons.

"You'll be smiling on the other side of your face when you see the headlines I mean," Scoop Slocum muttered as he turned and began running back to the newspaper office. For he had deceived Dan about the record book. He didn't have one. He was going back to the *Record* to write a story that would tell all about Dan Slade!

He was out of breath by the time he had pounded up the back stairs to the City Room and burst in upon an astounded John Artsen, the Night City Editor of the *Record*.

Mr. Artsen pushed back his green eyeshade and said, "You back again? I thought I told you to go home. You'd better have a world scoop or something."

For once, George Slocum had no swift retort on his lips. He hardly heard John Artsen's gibe as he ran to an unoccupied desk and sat down and started rolling a piece of yellow copy paper into a typewriter.

"You'll see, Mr. Artsen," he called.

"Now, Georgie," the Night City Editor said impatiently, "the sports page is closed. You can't get a story in 'Sports' until Sunday's paper."

"This," Scoop Slocum called over the racket his fingers were making with the typewriter keys, "is no story about sportsmanship!"

Shaking his head and smiling to himself, John Artsen pushed his eyeshade down over his eyes again and bent his head over the pile of copy on his desk. In a half hour, George was standing in front of him, trembling as he handed his story over to him.

"How's that for a Page One yarn?" little Scoop panted.

Mr. Artsen read, and as he did, his eyes went wide with interest. At last, he put it down and asked, "You want us to print this?"

"Of course!"

Mr. Artsen wagged his head in slow discouragement.

"We can't print this, boy."

"What? I thought this was a free country! I thought we had a free press!" Scoop was beside himself as he raged on. "Why can't you print it? It's true, I know it's true!"

"Maybe you do," Mr. Artsen said dryly. "But I don't. Why, Georgie, that boy's father could sue us for a million dollars if we printed that!"

"I don't care!" Scoop shrilled, losing his temper. "Every word of that is the truth. It's the truth, I tell you, the tr—"

"Here, here," a stern voice cut in. "What's all this racket out here?"

John Artsen's head bobbed like that of a frightened rabbit when he heard the familiar voice of Mr. William Madden, the publisher of the *Crawford Record*. He swallowed, and turned to see Mr. Madden coming out of his office with an expression of annoyance on his face.

"Oh, nothing, sir," Mr. Artsen said, gulping. "Sorry to have disturbed you so."

"Nothing, eh?" Mr. Madden grunted, cocking his silvery head to examine the abashed Scoop, standing in front of the City Desk. "I'd say that was certainly much ado about nothing. Well!" he said, shrugging, and made as though he would return to his office. And that was when Scoop took the boldest chance of his young life.

"Sir!" he cried, running after Mr. Madden. "It wasn't nothing! Here, read this!" He seized his rejected story from the hands of Mr. Artsen and thrust it at Mr. Madden. Startled, the publisher took it and read. His eyes, too, flew open. He stared thoughtfully at Scoop.

"Come with me," he said, and went into his office. "Are you sure of this?" he asked sternly, waving the story as Scoop followed him to his desk and stood there respectfully.

"Yes, sir," Scoop said.

"Tell me why you are."

Without hesitation, George Slocum launched into his story, and when he came to the part where he had seen the contract that had fallen out of Dan's coat pocket, Mr. Madden held up a hand and spoke sharply.

"Would you swear to that?"

"Yes, sir, I saw it!"

Shaking his head sorrowfully, Mr. Madden put the tips of his fingers together and leaned back in his chair. "Poor Owen Slade," he said. "His only son a spiteful sneak." He pulled himself heavily forward and reached for the telephone.

"You mean you *are* going to print my story, after all?" Scoop burst out eagerly.

Mr. Madden shook his head.

"I believe you, son. but I'm not going to print that story." As Scoop's face fell, the kindly publisher went on: "There are things called libel laws, boy. You may not understand them now, but you will later on." He lifted the telephone and began to dial. "But I'm going to do something better than printing it."

"What's that, sir."

"I'm going to talk to Owen Slade."

A broad smile creased Scoop's face, but then his face fell a second time as Mr. Madden spoke a few words into the telephone and hung up.

"Mr. Slade is out of town," he said. "But he'll be back tomorrow, and I'll speak to him then."

"What time, sir?"

"About noon."

Scoop groaned. "That's hardly more than an hour before game time! And we're playing in Crawford!"

Mr. Madden arose and held out his hand.

"I'm sorry, boy. I'm doing what I can to straighten this mess out for you. I've left word for Mr. Slade to call me as soon as he arrives. It's impossible to do more."

George Slocum took the publisher's hand and shook it warmly.

"Thank you, Mr. Madden, you've been swell!"

The publisher eyed him.

"You're not so bad yourself, young fellow. And if you should ever decide to make this kind of work a career, come and see me. I think we might make a newspaperman out of you."

Blushing, happy, slightly dazed, Scoop Slocum left the *Record* office and went home to bed.

CHAPTER FOURTEEN

A Wrong Righted

WIN HADLEY sat on the bench at Crawford Stadium, his head sunk in his hands and his eyes of a dullness to match the leaden sky overhead. The second half had only just begun, and already the Crawford Bisons were out in front, 13–0.

As Win Hadley sat sunk in gloom, his whole world seemed to be collapsing about him. Only that morning, he had had to watch his brother going down the front walk with slow and heavy step. Then he had had to watch Emil Okulski attempting to run the team against those hard-charging Bison linemen and their swift-tackling comrades in the secondary. Finally, and worst of all, he had had to look at Crawford's well-drilled offensive practically making mincemeat of the Dixboro line. There seemed to be absolutely no stopping that Ralph Bates, the short, stocky Bison quarterback who was as fast and tricky carrying the ball as he was sure and accurate passing it.

Bates was getting plenty of help from his big fullback, Fred Atchison. Coach Joyce had warned his Cougars about Atchison. "Hit him head-on, and low!" he had said. "If you don't, he'll trample you." Well, Atchison had done plenty of trampling already—and when he wasn't, Bates was throwing them to Bob Finch, a tricky end who seemed to pop up out of nowhere on the flanks.

The way Win Hadley felt, he almost wondered why he had bothered to put on a uniform. He had never felt so downcast, and he knew he had little desire to play football. But he wouldn't quit— never!

He looked down the bench and saw Dan Slade seated there. He looked glum too. Well, he should be, Win thought—after dropping the one good pass that Emil threw, and with a clear field ahead of him. To say nothing of the way he had been letting Bob Finch fake him out of his shoes. No wonder Coach Joyce took him out!

Well, it was all a sorry mess—and Dan Slade sure seemed to be spiting himself as well as everyone else with his mean little schemes of revenge.

There was a shout from the Crawford stands and a groan from the Dixboro bench, and Win Hadley saw that Ralph Bates had intercepted another of Emil's passes. That made three interceptions so far, and the end of the game was nowhere near! Behind him, Win heard the Cougar rooters starting to chant: "We want Hadley! We want Hadley!"

Somebody yelled angrily, "Hey, Joyce, what're you saving Hadley for—the Junior Prom?" and there were loud cries of agreement and a few cat-calls at the coach's expense. Win felt himself go hot with anger. Why make fun of the coach? He was doing what he thought was best for the team! Win started to steal a glance in the direction of Coach Joyce, and then, to his open-mouthed astonishment, he saw that the coach was on his feet, talking excitedly to somebody—and that somebody was no one else but Mr. Owen Slade!

In that instant, things began to go wild. First, there was the odd spectacle of little Scoop Slocum turning cartwheels on the side lines, pencil-and-paper-and-all, even though it was Crawford's ball on the Dixboro 47. Next, there was Coach Joyce whacking Mr. Slade on the back as though he were the star halfback being sent in to save the game. And, finally, there was a white-faced Mr. Slade striding purposefully over to his son Dan and talking to him in a manner that left no doubt that he was laying down the law about something. If Win blinked at this, he was utterly confounded at what happened next.

For once Mr. Slade had finished talking fiercely to his crestfallen son, he propelled him toward

Win Hadley, and there he brought him to a halt.

"Do as I said, confound it!" Mr. Slade snapped.

Looking as if he wished he could find a hole in the earth he could hide in, Dan Slade hung his head and muttered, "I—I'm sorry, Win."

"And so am I, boy," Mr. Slade added, looking directly at Win. "I'm sorry it had to be my son who has caused you so much distress. But your troubles are over now, boy. That contract is in your brother's hands right this minute—signed, sealed and delivered." Mr. Slade grinned and stepped back to let Win look over the fence to the spot in the stands where Walter stood, waving the contract in his hands and grinning happily.

Win Hadley's heart leaped for joy. In an instant, his world seemed whole again. He looked down the bench toward Coach Joyce, and Mr. Slade said, "That's right, boy. The coach wants to see you." He glanced severely at his son. "He wants you too, Dan—and remember, I'm going to be in those stands watching every move you make. Believe me, you'd better play the game right today!" With that, becoming embarrassed now that he had recovered his temper and realized that his strange behavior had caught the curiosity of thousands of people, Owen Slade cleared his throat nervously, adjusted his topcoat and left the side lines.

The two boys were standing in front of Coach Joyce.

"Ready to play again, Win?" Coach Joyce asked gently.

"Oh, yes, sir! You just watch!"

Tom Joyce grinned and patted him on the back. "Go in for Emil," he said.

A great shout rose from the Dixboro stands as Win Hadley's graceful figure was seen running onto the field.

"Well, now we're getting somewhere," the men remarked to one another.

On the bench, meanwhile, Coach Joyce was talking earnestly to Dan Slade.

"I've given you plenty of chances, Dan," he said grimly. "This one is the last. I've heard the whole miserable story from your father. By rights, I should suspend you from the squad. But I'm going to let you redeem yourself. Now, go in there and play football!"

Dan Slade sprinted out onto the field, and one of the Dixboro wags shouted in a high falsetto voice, "Here comes Danny Butterfingers."

Dan Slade's face was red as a beet by the time he took up his position on the right wing, but he silenced the grandstand wiseacre forever on the next play. Seeing Dan back in the game, the clever Ralph Bates had called for a down-and-out pass to Bob Finch in Dan's territory. But Dan was doing some thinking, too—straight thinking of the kind he had almost forgotten about. He guessed that Bates would test him, and when Bob Finch had finished faking left and darted right to receive the pass, he found the black-shirted Cougar back was there before him!

A second after he had caught the ball, Dan was buried under a swarm of white jerseys and red pants as the infuriated Bisons hit him from every side. But Dan Slade got up grinning. He cast a mocking glance at the grandstand, and then he raced back to the huddle.

"Nice going, Dan!" Win Hadley called, slapping his erstwhile enemy on the back. "Let's whittle 'em."

"Right!" Dan said, his eyes sparkling. "I said before I was sorry. Now, I'm going to show you!"

"Dearie me," Red McGinley simpered. "Aren't those two just ducky!"

The entire team grinned in the huddle and, with that, the gloom of defeat seemed to vanish as a fresh wave of fighting spirit swept over them.

"Okay!" Win snapped. "Up the middle. Teddy, on a count of three!"

They broke from the huddle yipping with their old pep, and Win Hadley exulted as he slammed the ball into Teddy's belly and watched the fullback churn for yardage behind the driving Archie, Bill Keller and Matt Hughes. It was the Cougars' first real gain of the day, and the Bisons were so surprised they couldn't pull the chunky Dixboro fullback down until he had bulled for twelve yards.

First and ten, Dixboro's ball on the midfield stripe!

"That's the way! Let's sock it to 'em," Win Hadley hissed as they huddled once again. He craned his head for a look at the Crawford defenses and saw that the left end seemed to be playing wide. "Keeper right, count of five. Watch for the lateral, Dan."

Dan nodded, and as Win counted to two, he drifted off in motion to his right. At five, Win had the ball and was running low behind the line. He saw that the Crawford end had outguessed him and was coming in fast to nail him. He leaped and threw to Dan. The end scrambled back, but it appeared that Dan would get around him. Then, Win Hadley heard Dan calling, "Quick, Win—a lateral!"

Swiftly, Win cut wide to outflank Dan, and as he did, the fleet Dixboro halfback shoveled the ball backward into Win's outstretched arms and threw himself at the Crawford linebacker coming up fast. Dan Slade burst on that poor Bison tackler like a bomb. He just blotted him out, and left Win Hadley as pretty a downfield avenue as any ball-carrier could ask for.

Dan Slade had never given up a chance to shine before in his life, and this time, he not only did that, but he threw a block as well.

And Win Hadley showed his appreciation.

CHAPTER FIFTEEN

Victory Play

WIN HADLEY sprinted goalward, gathering blockers. He was hardly conscious of the swelling thun-
der of voices breaking from the Dixboro stands as
he did his tightrope walk down the side lines. At
the Crawford 40, big Fred Atchison dived at him
and got his arms around his waist. But Win whirled
like a dancer and the Bison fullback was thrown a
half dozen feet into the Dixboro bench. Now, Win
was at the Crawford 30, and all alone but for Ralph
Bates coming over fast and trying to force him into
a box—so that he'd be trapped somewhere about
the 15.

Win slowed his pace just the tiniest trifle, and as
the powerful Crawford quarterback came toward
him, running low and eying him warily, Win suddenly turned on the steam, reversed his field,

shifted the ball from right hand to left and planted a strong, stiff straight-arm right in Bates's startled face. He left him sprawled on the 18 behind him and he crossed the Crawford goal line standing up!

At last, Dixboro had something to make a noise about.

And how they cheered! Even the strains of the Dixboro Victory March were drowned out in that storm of cheers that came down from the black-and-gold bannered Cougar stands. Then, as the teams lined up for the extra point, the jubilant fans quieted down. But the storm broke out afresh as big Matt booted the ball squarely between the uprights.

Crawford 13, Dixboro 7—and the big score-board clock showed that there were five minutes remaining in the third period.

On the kickoff, Matt Hughes was so happy he kicked the ball into the Crawford end zone.

"Come on, fellows, let's rack 'em up," he shouted as the black-and-gold gridders got down on their hands and knees to halt the first Bison rush.

It was big Fred Atchison carrying. He came up the middle on a draw play and big Matt met him squarely at the line of scrimmage.

Smack!

Clear up in the stands, old-time footballers shivered at the sound of an impact that they could feel in their own bones.

Matt Hughes sprang to his feet, joyfully shouting, "See what I mean? You guys have just been making 'em look good!"

The big Crawford backfield star didn't get up so happily. He staggered erect, shook his head as though to clear it, took a faltering half-step toward the Dixboro line, but then changed his mind and walked slowly to his own huddle.

"Watch him!" Archie Campbell called. "He may be faking."

But he wasn't. The next play was a bootleg run by Ralph Bates. The Crawford quarter feinted to Atchison, lumbering up the middle, then stuck the ball behind his back to hide it and rolled out to his left. He ran into a reception committee composed of Al Jacobson, Win Hadley and Gabby Windham—and he went down for a loss of five yards.

By this point, the Dixboro stands were almost uncontrollable, hardly heeding the cheerleaders as they chanted: "Push 'em back, push 'em back, push 'em back—FARTHER!"

On the next play, the Crawford quarterback showed just how cagey he was. With third and fifteen to go on his own 15, he lined up in a straight T-formation. At the count of two he jumped and parted his legs and the center passed directly to Atchison, who had taken two backward steps. Atchison quick-kicked it.

The ball shot downfield with Dan Slade flying after it.

He scooped it up on the run as he hit his own 35, but this time there were no Fancy Dan tactics of continuing to go backward to look for more running room and a grandstand punt return. No, Dan Slade stopped short, got away from one tackler, and then fought his way upfield until he had brought the ball back to the Dixboro 45.

Up in the stands, Owen Slade smiled his first smile of the day. Beside him, Walter Hadley tapped his shoulder and said, "Ten mighty important yards, I'd say, Mr. Slade. And he got them the hard way."

Down on the field, Win Hadley was finding that the Crawford linemen were over their surprise and were really digging in.

On the first play, he ran a keeper left. He went down under a pile of white jerseys before he had taken two steps, and when he got to his feet, he saw that he had lost two yards. In the huddle, he called for a shovel pass to Dan, hoping that the Bison ends would not be so tough. But as the teams lined up, and Win went into his long count, he saw why he had been spilled so quickly. The Crawford men were shifting into a seven-man line. Desperately, he glanced over the backs of his crouching linemen and caught the eye of Al Jacobson. Al winked. He had seen it, too.

The moment Win got the ball, the Crawford men charged. But Al had scooted quickly into the slot over center and Win jumped and hit him with a pass. Al legged it to the Crawford 47 before they nailed him.

Third down, two to go—and there was the gun ending the third quarter.

Now, the trailing Dixboro Cougars had only twelve minutes left in which to tie the score or go out in front.

But Win Hanley knew in his heart just how difficult that was going to be. Crawford's tough, smart gridders wouldn't be caught napping again, as they had been on Win's touchdown scamper. No, if the Cougars were going to cross the Bison goal again, they were going to have to grind it out. It would take short gains of four and five yards. Win looked at his teammates. He was glad they were in good condition, and he was gladder still that he had just the right offensive system to grind out a steady march. That was the keeper play!

As they huddled to start the final quarter, Win said, "All right, this it it, gang! And it's going to be the keeper all the way!" He stared at big Archie and Matt and Bill Keller. "It's up to you three," he said with quiet emphasis. "If you let them get through, we're done." He smacked his hands together and said, "So let's roll! Al, take three steps again. Maybe we can cross them up a second time. Okay, gang—on three!"

A great cheer of encouragement broke from the Dixboro rooting section as their gallant black-and-gold heroes fairly raced from the huddle to the line of scrimmage. The drum beat crazily and the bugler got off a long, rising trumpet call.

"Signals: one, two, three—"

The ball was in Win Hadley's hand. He looked quickly for Al Jacobson and groaned. The end had slipped and was lying flat on the ground. The Crawford secondary had Dan covered completely, and in another second or so, Archie and Matt and Bill would have to go down before the linemen who were hand-fighting them with savage determination. Win was about to tuck the ball into his belly and try to buck the line, when he heard Dan yell at him and saw that he had the end boxed. Quickly, Win lit out for the side lines. He didn't get too far, because he was run out of bounds on the Crawford 45, but he had just made the first down.

On the next play, Win sent Gabby into the left side of the line, "just to keep 'em honest," and then tried the keeper right again, with Dan doing a ballet dance through the Crawford secondary for six big yards. Then, he kept it himself and cut back between tackle and guard. He got five yards and another first down. But he had had to fight for them, and he knew that Crawford would be jamming it up again.

"Watch for the pass, Al," he panted in the huddle, and got himself set under center once more.

He took the ball, and was almost instantly buried under a host of Bison tacklers. A five-yard loss!

"Give it to me this time, Win!" Dan Slade pleaded in the huddle. "I've got that Crawford end in my back pocket."

Win nodded. Then he had another thought.

"No," he said. "I mean, yes. I'll lateral it to you, but you pass it to Al. You haven't passed all season. Once you get the ball, they'll be positive that you're going to run, and they'll close up."

"Right," Dan said, and as they lined up, a hush fell over the field. Everyone in the stands knew that this was a key play. Second down and fifteen yards to go. If the Cougars didn't bite off yardage on this try, they'd be in a bad way.

Slowly, Win Hadley barked out his signals. He took the ball, ran to his right, made as though to slant inside tackle—and then shoveled the ball out to Dan. The Dixboro speedster lowered his head and took off.

"Get him! Get him!" shouted the Crawford defenders, and they streamed to their left, determined to box Dan in before he could "turn the corner." But the moment Dan neared the side lines, he braked to a halt and raised his right arm for a pass. Crawford was completely fooled, and only a quick recovery by Ralph Bates kept Al Jacobson from going the distance, once he had gathered Dan's wobbly pass into his arms.

The Dixboro fans were screaming with joy as the referee placed the ball down on the Crawford 32 and made the signal for a first down!

The din was almost deafening as they chanted, over and over: "Touchdown, touchdown—we want a touchdown!"

Grimly, Win Hadley got under the center. He grasped the ball and got his knees churning under him. A determined Bison bore down on him. Win swung his arms as though shoveling the ball out again, feinted wide to his right, and then whirled inside the tackler. He could have laughed at the expression of surprise on the Crawford man's face as he lost his balance and his legs shot out from under him. But two seconds later, Win felt far from laughter. Big Fred Atchison had caught Win's right arm as the Dixboro quarterback tried to straight-arm him, and he gave it a ferocious yank as he dragged Win to the gridiron.

Though the fans were yelling again, and though he knew he had picked up eight important yards, Win Hadley lay on the ground groaning to himself. His right shoulder felt as though it were on fire. He knew, without making the attempt, that he would never be able to raise it to throw a pass, and without that possibility, half of the keeper play's effectiveness was canceled out! Of course, he could still lateral, though it would hurt—but without the threat of the pass to Al Jacobson, things were going to be tough.

He got quickly to his feet, anxious to keep his injury a secret. But Matt Hughes had seen him wince as he was flung to the ground, and he was boiling with anger as they huddled again.

"The dirty ape!" he growled. "He did it on purpose. Your arm okay, Win?"

Win shook his head, and the team nearly groaned aloud.

"I can fake it, though," he said. "And when we want a pass, I'll lateral out to Dan."

Matt Hughes ground his teeth together.

"Run one at that ape again, Win," he snarled. "I'll lead the play."

Win Hadley grinned at the sight of his friend's angry face.

"Okay," he said, smacking his hands together. "You lead me home, Matt."

Big Matt was growling in his chest as they lined up for the next play. The opposing Crawford lineman never knew what hit him when Matt struck him fiercely amidships, and then barreled into the secondary to square accounts with the dirty-playing Crawford fullback. Win Hadley was right behind him, having ducked back into the line on the keeper. He saw Matt bearing down on Atchison, who was rushing in to plug the gap, and he cut to his left.

Matt left his feet.

Crash!

Atchison crumpled and sank to the earth.

Win raced laterally for a six-yard gain before he was run out of bounds by Bates. When he turned around to run back to the huddle, he wasn't surprised to see that Atchison was still lying on the ground. Time out was called, while the doctor and the Crawford coach ran out onto the field to the aid of their star fullback. But Matt had only knocked the wind out of him, and within another minute, Atchison was sucking big mouthfuls of air into his lungs and putting on his helmet. But when he took up his position again, he had the look of a man who wished the final whistle would blow.

"That'll teach the dirty ape!" Matt shouted in the huddle, raising his voice to be heard above the roar of the Dixboro stands calling for the Cougars to cover the remaining twenty yards to the Crawford goal.

And those twenty yards cost the Cougars plenty. They had to fight every step of the way, and there was no repetition of Win's sensational dash of the period before. First, Gabby Windham ran the dive play for three. Then, Teddy Scholari bucked for two. Win ran the keeper for four more, and then, calling for a quarterback sneak, he had to carry the entire center of the Crawford line on his shoulders just to pick up that precious last yard. But he made it.

There was a long anxious moment while the linemen brought in the chains, and what a shout of delight broke from the Cougar side of the field when the referee signaled the first down!

But, now, Crawford was playing an eight-man line. It was going to be suicide to try to run through that defense.

"Jump pass to Red," Win called in the huddle, and his teammates looked at him in astonishment.

"Are you okay, Win?" Archie Campbell asked anxiously. "I mean, your arm . . . you said you couldn't pass."

Win gritted his teeth.

"I've got to try it. We've got to open 'em up."

Maybe I can get just one off, Win thought as he ran back to the line of scrimmage. I've just got to.

But he couldn't. The moment he leaped in the air and brought his hand back to throw, such a tongue of flame ran through his arm that he nearly cried aloud in pain. The best he could do was cuddle the ball and scramble back to the line of scrimmage. No gain.

There was a deep groan from the Dixboro stands. But Win had not lost heart, and he still had his wits about him. Somehow or other, the Bisons had to be convinced that he would try a pass again. As he spoke to the team in the huddle, Win made a big show of wiping his hands on his pants. As they lined up, he let his eyes stray downfield and, once, he glanced nervously over at Al Jacobson. Then he took the ball and faded back. The Crawford secondary began to back-pedal frantically.

And Win Hadley handed off to Teddy Scholari on the draw play!

For one long moment, no one within Crawford Stadium but Win and Teddy seemed to know where the ball was. And then, as the Bison linemen came charging toward him, making for Win Hadley—Teddy Scholari drove forward like a shot. One man got a hand on him at the line of scrimmage, but he only served to increase Teddy's momentum. He tripped him, yes, but when the next tackler came up to stop Teddy, the chunky fullback was staggering forward at such a rate that the collision helped him to regain his balance. In another instant, Teddy had crossed the final chalk line and the place went mad.

It was 13–13, all tied up, and now the best placekicker in the League was in a position to put Dixboro out in front.

A deep silence fell as the Cougars lined up.

The ball came back to Win. He placed it.

Matt Hughes ran up and kicked it.

And he missed!

The ball went to the left of the goal posts. It was the first time that season that Matt had actually missed a kick—and at what a time!

There were actual tears in big Matt's eyes as he trudged upfield for the kickoff. Over and over, he kept saying, "I lost the game, I lost the game." Win ran up and pounded him on the shoulders and said, "Stop blubbering, you big booby. You didn't lose any game. There's still six minutes to go!" Win grinned. "I'll bet you can't make 'em fumble the kickoff," he taunted.

"Oh, no?" Matt growled, forgetting his sorrow.

He trotted downfield and booted the ball down to the 7 and he raced after it like a trailer-truck rolling down a hill without brakes.

The ball was taken by Ralph Bates, and Ralph Bates was taken by Matt Hughes.

The big Cougar tackle sailed into the Bison ball-carrier and the football popped high into the air.

"Fumble!" the players roared, and then there occurred one of those freak plays that make the game of football so exciting and unpredictable.

Bates had been running to his right when Matt hit him. When the ball spurted from his arms, it went to the left. Also going left at the time was the Crawford end, Bob Finch. He caught the fumble, and because he was going to the left when he caught it, he also crossed up the entire Dixboro team.

The Cougars could not recover in time.

By the time they had reversed their field and regained their balance, Finch was halfway to the goal with three blockers ahead of him. Only Win Hadley stood between them and the touchdown, and when he flung himself at the interference in a desperate attempt to break up the play, Finch coolly slowed down, hurdled the pile-up and proceeded on his way untouched.

Dixboro was stunned.

Hardly a minute before, the game had been tied. Now, it was Crawford 19, Dixboro 13—and there weren't many people who took comfort from the fact that Archie Campbell, Matt Hughes and Charley Bantam overwhelmed Ralph Bates's extra point attempt with a furious charge.

On the bench, Coach Tom Joyce was shaking his head sorrowfully.

"A football sure takes some crazy bounces," he muttered to Jocko Williams, and the usually cheerful assistant could do little more than nod a gloomy assent.

Crawford's kickoff went to Dan Slade, and Dan raced back to the Dixboro 35 before he was brought low on a shoestring tackle by Bob Finch.

Win tried running the keeper on the first play. But Crawford was still jamming up the forward wall and he could get only three yards. Win called time out.

"Funny," he said, frowning, as he knelt on the gridiron with the team. "You'd think they'd be playing us deep for the long passes. But they're jamming it up."

"I think they've guessed about your arm," Dan Slade said. "You may not know it yourself, but you've been holding it kind of stiff. That guy Bates has been watching you like a hawk. I think they know."

Win Hadley frowned again.

"But we've got to open them up! Here, I'll lateral to you, Dan, and you throw 'em."

Dan Slade shrugged.

"Okay by me. But you know I'm no passer."

Dan proved his point on the next two plays. Both times he took a lateral from Win and went wide on the pass-run option. Both times, he had Al Jacobson in the clear, and both times he missed the mark. The first one was so weak and wobbly it fell harmlessly to the ground. On the second, he threw so hard it sailed over Al's head and was almost intercepted by Ralph Bates.

Gloomily, Win Hadley went back to kick. He looked at the clock. Four minutes to play!

The football came spiraling back to him and he got his foot into the ball.

Bates signaled for a fair catch on his own 25 and caught the ball neatly.

Now, the Dixboro stands were really sunk in despair.

For, as everyone expected, Crawford deliberately began to "eat the clock." Ralph Bates didn't even take the chance of handing the ball off. On the first play, he merely took it, wrapped his arms around it and knelt down. He might have done that on two more plays, and then kicked, had not Charley Bantam been offside. That gave the Bisons a first-and-five situation, and they had no trouble picking up five more for the first down on their own 35.

Two and a half minutes to go!

Bates went back to his earlier tactics. Three times he took the ball and knelt down, and he was awfully lazy about calling his plays. When he finally dropped back to punt, standing on his own 20, there was only a minute and three seconds left.

Bates took no chances with Dan Slade either. He deliberately angled for the side lines, and because he was the kind of "money player" who always rises to an occasion, he planted it out of bounds on the Dixboro 40.

Crawford rooters roared their approval of that masterly kick, and there wasn't a peep from the other side of the field where the black-and-gold pennants seemed to droop in defeat.

Dan Slade was grinding his teeth in a despairing rage when the Cougars huddled. He had hoped to run the ball back for a touchdown. If only he could get out in the open, he told himself. Just a half step —that's all he ever needed to break away. Dan was unaware that Win Hadley was studying him and was thinking exactly the same thing.

Only Dan can do it now, Win thought. Only he had the speed to cover those discouraging sixty yards to the goal line. But, what to do? Crawford was certainly going to play in close again, not fearing Win's passes. How break Dan loose?

Win Hadley had an inspiration. He remembered the play that they had been rehearsing all week, the double reverse with a lateral. The only thing was, it ended with Win carrying the ball. But he could change that!

Win looked at the clock.

Fifty seconds left!

"There's just time for two plays," he panted quickly in the huddle. "So listen: on the first, we'll run a keeper to the right, just to set up running room to the left. Then, we'll line up again. But just before signals, Dan, you change places with me and—"

"Huh?" Dan Slade said, astounded, but Win waved him into silence and hurried on.

"Yes, that's right. We'll use that reverse-lateral play, but this time, Dan will be getting the ball—

not me." He looked hard at Dan. "Think you can do it?"

Dan grinned. "Lead me to it," he said.

They broke from the huddle and lined up.

On a quick count, Win took the ball and ran to the right. He went down, as expected, for no gain. He felt a sharp pain jab his arm. Quickly, he scrambled erect, glancing at the scoreboard.

Thirty seconds!

As Win ran to the line of scrimmage, he passed Matt Hughes.

"It's up to you to take out Bates," he said to him. "If he's still on his feet back there, Dan'll never make it."

Matt nodded and went down into his offensive crouch.

A groan of dismay rose from the Dixboro stands as Win and Dan quickly changed places. "Cut the sand-lot stuff, Dixboro!" someone shouted furiously, and then there was an even louder groan as the fans saw the play developing.

Dan took the snap from Archie and handed off to Win going left. Win was almost knocked off his feet by the lineman who had filtered through the gap left by Matt charging downfield for Ralph Bates. But he stayed on his feet and handed off to Gabby going to the right. That was when the groans came. For it looked as if Gabby was going to run into a wall of Crawford tacklers. The Bisons streamed in that direction, and no one paid the slightest attention to Dan Slade. He seemed out of the play.

Then, Dan got going.

Gabby whirled and flipped to him.

There was a roar of amazement from both stands.

By the time Dan had caught the ball he already had three strides on the completely outfoxed Crawford team.

His legs fairly twinkled as he streaked down the side lines. And then he shifted into high. He had reached midfield before Crawford seemed to guess what had happened, and as Win Hadley sped downfield after him, he saw that only Ralph Bates remained in the play.

And big Matt was bearing down on him.

But Bates was not to be taken out so easily. He hand-fought Matt down the side lines, ducking this way and that, cleverly trying to slow Dan so that someone could come up from behind to make the tackle. And Win saw that Bates's strategy was going to succeed. Even though Matt finally bowled him over as Dan reached the 35, Bates had slowed the Dixboro speedster down so much that Dan had to cut to his right to avoid tacklers coming up behind him.

And that meant that Bob Finch, tearing down the right side line, was going to have time to overtake Dan before he could turn it on again.

Running hard, Win swerved and tried to place himself between Finch and Dan.

But he would never make it. Though his breath came sobbingly as he tried to muster an extra burst of speed, he knew that he would not catch Finch. Dixboro's only hope was that Dan's returning speed would carry him over the goal line before Finch hit him.

But Dan Slade didn't figure it that way.

Seeing Win coming up behind him, he gasped, "Lateral," stopped dead, threw the ball to Win going by him to the left, and then knocked Finch sprawling.

Win Hadley caught the ball and galloped over the goal line with the tying touchdown.

Up in the stands, Walter Hadley was pounding Owen Slade on the back with all his might. But Mr. Slade hardly felt it, and he hardly saw the field where the delirious players were hugging Dan and Win and jumping up and down with joy. That was because his eyes were misty with tears.

"What a play!" Walter Hadley shouted over the bedlam around him, throwing up a hand to keep the paper streamers and confetti out of his eyes. "Did you see that run? Did you see that lateral? Did you see that block? Boy, oh, boy—what a play!"

Owen Slade blew his nose.

Then, in the hush that lay over Crawford Stadium, Matt Hughes calmly stepped up to the ball held by Win Hadley and booted it neatly between the uprights.

The gun went off as Ralph Bates was tackled on his own 35 while returning the kickoff, and in an instant, the field was alive with the substitute Dixboro players and the fans who had swarmed from their seats. And that was how the game ended: Dixboro 20, Crawford 19.

Win Hadley grinned with delight at the sight of the Crawford goal posts going down and a happy Dan Slade going up on the shoulders of his overjoyed townsmen. Then, to Win's surprise, he felt himself going up on their shoulders, too—and there was Matt Hughes getting the same kind of triumphant ride to the dressing room.

Watching them, his eager face split from side to side in a happy grin, was little George Slocum.

"Hot diggety!" he shouted, catching sight of Owen Slade and Walter Hadley. "I'll bet we win the League and go undefeated this season!"

"You know, son," Mr. Slade said, grinning himself, "I think you may be a prophet, after all."

And, as it turned out, he was.